My E~~est Friend is Mean~~

A Collection of Reader-Submitted Medical Stories

Kerry Hamm

Disclaimer:

Names, locations, and portions of the
details included in this book have been altered
to protect the privacy of those involved.

<u>Warning:</u>

This edition features light profanity that may be offensive to some readers. The profanity has been used sparingly and in each instance the usage was included in the submission. I have chosen to leave some of these words in to emphasize portions of the stories.

By now, I am sure you are all too familiar with my *Real Stories from a Small-Town ER* series, which were collections of stories told to you from my time as a registration clerk in Ohio. If you are new here, don't fret! You don't have to worry about a 'certain order' for *any* of my books, including this one!

I have since moved on from the hospital scene, but that hasn't stopped readers from submitting stories of their own experiences from the medical field. Over time, I have received hundreds of stories-some funny, some sad, some downright scary or grotesque-and have worked with my readers to bring these stories to you in a follow up to my last *Real Stories* volume.

If I've learned anything from writing my series and compiling this book, it's that none of us are alone. We're all proof that we've seen some seriously messed up things out there, right? We have seen the good. We've seen the bad. We've seen the downright vile and disgusting. And then, we've seen the humor in these situations and we've been fortunate enough to share them with one another. There is a certain peace in knowing that as no matter how crazy we feel, we have formed solidarity amongst ourselves, knowing that for every bad day you've had, others have had them too. We have worked through the challenges of getting up and facing another drug seeker, another child abuse case, another young death, and another 'how the heck did that even happen?' moment together. You guys are not alone, and this book reaffirms that.

Several of the stories have been edited to bring you clear-cut and clean versions of tales submitted by loyal readers. I have done my very best to edit out hospital and town names, and in some cases my submitters wished to withhold their initials and other details from publication or requested that I edit stories for grammar/spelling. Some stories have been edited for length. I do my very best to preserve a reader's humor and emotions, as well as capture the reader's personality when I edit these submissions. To be clear, I do my best to remove ANY identifying information from these submissions, and sometimes that may include altering specific stand-out details with the submitter's permission. This is to prevent readers from searching for patients online, thus revealing the identities of parties involved. This is done carefully, and I work with readers to keep touchy submissions as close to the initial submission as possible.

Though some of the stories in this collection are horrifying, I am glad none of us are alone in what we've witnessed or experienced.

(

<u>Cheat Sheet</u>

Some readers have been confused about terms used in this series. Here's a quick list to help you out!

LEO: Law Enforcement Officer

ETOH: shorthand for Ethyl Alcohol or Ethanol; commonly used to describe intoxicated individuals

Bus/Rig/Truck: Ambulance

M.D.: Medical Doctor

R.N.: Registered Nurse

MVA: Motor Vehicle Accident

EMS: Emergency Medical Services

EMT: Emergency Medical Technician

PD/FD: Police Department/Fire Department

D.A.: District Attorney

BOLO: Be on (the) Lookout

DCFS/CPS: Department of Children and Family Services/Child Protective Services

SNF: Skilled Nursing Facility. This can be a nursing home or one of many facilities for patients in need of supervised care

AMA: Against Medical Advice

LWBS/LBT: Left Without Being Seen/Left Before Triage

LOL: Little Old Lady

<u>Oops</u>

It was a particularly rough winter, and one that seemed to go on forever. That year, our first snowstorm came the day before Halloween, and with each passing month Mother Nature seemed to taunt us, asking, "Oh, want some more, huh?"

We rolled into a new year, but the biting temps and mounds of snow were still there and in full force. What's worse was that on a Friday night, Mother Nature took a pause from sending us snow and decided to throw a rainstorm our way. As I'm sure you've guessed by now, all that rain froze over, and all the roads were makeshift ice rinks. Schools, churches, and sports organizations canceled their weekend events. The roads were so bad that even fast food joints, grocery stores, and movie theaters shut down for the weekend. Our small, rural town became even more quiet as residents hunkered down in their homes.

As we all know, healthcare professionals do not have the luxury of staying home during inclement weather. When I woke up that evening, I peeked out the window. My girlfriend was admiring the freshly-fallen six-inches of snow that had come down while I was asleep. I, on the other hand, cursed under my breath before proceeding to get ready for work.

Surprisingly, my partner and I were only dispatched to three runs in the span of a four-hour period. The calls were legitimate medical crises for the patients involved. Unfortunately, we lost one of the patients en route to the ER, as we could not safely maintain vehicle speeds over 15 MPH. Even 15 MPH was pushing it, and on several roads we had to slow to 5 MPH and pray that we could even pass on that road.

My partner and I lounged around the station for a while. At 03:00, we were dispatched to the ER, this time for a transport. We were responsible for transporting a corpse to the morgue, which was located across town.

Well, in this area, when you have to pick up a body, you have to drive around to the back of the facility, which is located on somewhat of an incline. Ordinarily, the doughnut drive is easy to navigate, and crews are in and out of there in about 5-10 minutes, depending on paperwork, chit-chat, those sorts of things. We did have concerns about navigating the driveway before we even set out for the hospital, but the facility's on-duty supervisor very sternly informed us that there were no other authorized loading locations and that we had little choice in the matter.

Upon arriving at the hospital, we concluded that our concerns had been valid. We were experiencing difficulty right off the bat when it came to climbing the incline. My partner would give the rig a bit of gas, but we'd slide back almost instantly. It took us six minutes just to make it to the top of the drive.

One thing the hospital failed to mention was that the patient's family wanted to 'say goodbye.' We quickly learned that the elderly couple had not spent a single day apart in more than 15 years, so the separation was especially hard on our patient's widow, a tiny, teary-eyed woman who stood under the awning as chunky snowflakes caked her three scarves, bulky bubble jacket, and even began covering the toes of her winter boots.

We loaded the patient in the back of the rig and tried to take off, but we couldn't move. Imagine that.

Luckily, a security officer carried a bag of cat litter in his trunk and hauled it around for us. My partner thought I put the litter down already, so he kept giving the rig gas & we couldn't hear each other through shouts or through our radios (because of the engine), so I thought the best logical way to handle this would be to open the rig doors and yell to the front when it was time to tell my partner to give the rig gas.

I poured the litter around the tires and called through the rig for my partner to hit the gas. The wheels spun, but the rig didn't move. No big deal. We didn't expect it to work on the first time. I *did* expect it to work on the second. Or third. Or fourth. It didn't.

We decided to give it one more try, so I used the entire bag of litter around the tires and called out for my partner to give the rig gas. Finally, the rig moved. Unfortunately, it only went about a foot and then stalled.

In this moment, with a security officer, orderly, and elderly woman watching, the gurney inside rolled back (from the rig jerking around), knocked me over, and went sliding down the hill. I'm talking, this gurney just went zig-zagging all over the place. It was zipping down the hill so quickly that all I could really make out was the blue blur of the body bag. Zoooom, it was gone. The gurney flipped twice and somehow landed upright in an embankment, with our deceased patient still strapped to it. My partner didn't know that we'd lost our patient, so he kept giving the rig gas. When I grabbed one of the swinging doors and attempted to pull myself up, the rig actually moved and dragged me about six feet with it.

I was fine. I had a few bruises and minor scrapes, but I was honestly more concerned with our patient and the fact that his widow had witnessed the entire incident. I rushed over to apologize and console her because she appeared to be sobbing, but upon closer examination we all realized she was laughing.

"He always liked to go sledding," she cackled. "He must have wanted to go one last time."

She was laughing so hard that we had to administer oxygen and she was taken to the ER for a quick once-over. She assured everyone involved that she was not angry about what had occurred and that "It's just like [her husband] to make a scene."

We—the hospital, my partner, and I— were afraid we would be sued over the incident. Nothing ever came of it.

Following that incident, the hospital changed their procedures and they now allow for front-facility loading, where the ground is flat and there is no risk of a corpse sliding down the hill.

-M.L.
Michigan

Daddy Daughter Time

My husband had been gone on a business trip for 11 days, so my 2-year-old daughter and I were thrilled to have him home. I believe I may have been slightly more excited to have him home than she was because I work night shift in Lab and often work 12-hour shifts or longer. Toddlers don't care if you've been up all night. My daughter began her days between 05:00 and 06:00, and since she was in a defiant stage and loved to fight every authority figure on every matter, the days felt even longer.

I hadn't been able to nap that day, and my back had been killing me. My husband came home just a few hours before I was scheduled for a shift, and thankfully, he took my daughter out for a daddy-daughter date at McDonald's.

The man must have given her too much sugar or something, because when they came home, our daughter was running around the house like she was Speedy Gonzales.

I was using my last bit of energy to lie on the floor and force myself to do my exercise video. That's only partial true. I basically got in position to do sit ups, but my back felt so good stretched out on the hard floor, so I was lying on the floor and watching these incredibly fit women jump around like they were immune to breathlessness and thigh cramps.

"Chris," I begged my husband, "can you please keep her out of the way until I'm done?"

My husband chased our daughter around the house and then lifted her up on his shoulders. Before I could even remind him that the ceiling fan was on, one of the blades whacked my daughter in the forehead and she went flying off his shoulders.

You're probably thinking this is a story about rushing my child to the ER for a gash in her forehead or something of the sort, but not quite. You see, I broke her fall. Her torso landed on my upper chest, and her pelvic area landed directly on my face. Essentially, I was hit in the face by a 23-pound flying sugar-high.

At first, I was so worried about her safety that I didn't realize I was in excruciating pain. I tried to sit up to examine her, but I couldn't get up on my own. My husband barreled in and swept her up, but she didn't have a mark on her. In fact, she was giggling.

"Oh my God," said my husband, "your nose is bleeding."

I remember asking him to get me a towel or something, so *of course* he comes back with the decorative kitchen towels I bought off Etsy for $42. I wasn't even paying enough attention to be able to tell him, "No, grab something else."

He helped me sit up, and the pain was even worse. We couldn't get my nose to stop bleeding, and it hurt to breathe.

"I'm gonna call 911," my husband said.

"Don't you dare call 911," I said. I had tried to yell, but it hurt so much that my voice came out as a whimper.

"You can drive us," I said.

Ever tried to leave your house when you have a toddler? My daughter was not only taking the most inopportune time to play 'run away from daddy,' but she was also stripping her clothes off as she was going. My husband was trying to bribe her like he does with the dogs when they don't listen in the yard, so he was using a too-sweet voice and asking, "Do you want a candy? Do you want a toy?"

"Chris," I cried, "you're gonna have to use your mad voice."

Somehow, in the middle of me needing to go to the hospital, we entered a parenting discussion that pretty much became instant bickering.

I think some key phrases involved in this spat were, "Well how would you know? You've been gone for two weeks," and, "Well, do you think that's maybe why she only listens to me?" I'm sure there were some curse words thrown in there.

The dogs came in from outside, and my now-naked toddler was within arm's reach. I was able to grab her. My husband put her clothes back on, and we loaded into the car about 20-25 minutes after this all happened. My nose was still bleeding, and by this point, it looked like someone had thrown a bucket of blood down the front of my shirt. I couldn't sit up straight in the car, but it hurt to slouch. My daughter screamed her head off in the backseat because I made my husband take away a shoelace she'd found and was putting in her mouth, and my husband was panicking as he was driving, so it was like we were in Daytona 500: Road Rage edition.

I was actually in the ER past the point that my shift was scheduled, so it was safe to say that my supervisor and coworkers were well aware that I would not be at work that night…at least not in a working sense.

I suffered from what my husband likes to call 'The Great Toddler Rampage of 2017,' and I was treated for a broken nose, a displaced rib, as well as two cracked ribs.

I was pretty bruised and sore for a while, so I ended up taking a bit of time off work. On day 2 ½ of my husband the only one taking care of our daughter, he came upstairs where I was recuperating in bed, plopped down next to me, and he said, "I don't know how you do it. It just took an hour and a half to put her down for a nap, and she learned a new cuss word."

Parenting sure isn't for the weak.

I ended up recovering just fine, but my daughter was having fun with her newly-discovered four-letter curse word, so that was another headache.

-H.J.
Alabama

<u>Meet the Parents</u>

When I was in med school, I met this
gorgeous girl I'll never forget. She was
everything I could've asked for: beautiful,
smart, funny, brave. It was a different time
back then, so when I told my friends I wanted
to marry this woman after dating for only two
weeks, they thought I was insane. Still, I
withdrew my entire savings account—money
that I'd been saving from mowing lawns and
bussing tables since the age of 15—and I
bought the biggest, nicest engagement ring I
could find.

My girlfriend wanted me to meet her
parents, so I'd planned it all out in my head
that we would get through supper, and then I
would ask my girl if she wanted to take a
walk. We would go to the park where we'd
met, and I would propose to her there. She'd
say yes, and then we'd gleefully skip back to
her home, where she'd deliver the great news.
Her parents would be thrilled and immediately

refer to me as their son, and oh boy, it would be great.

The big night arrived, and I straightened my dinner jacket as I waited for someone to answer the front door.

"So you must be the boyfriend," my girlfriend's mother snidely commented. She looked me over and rolled her eyes before walking away.

That certainly wasn't the response for which I'd been hoping, but I thought things would go better during supper. Instead, things got worse. Much worse.

My girlfriend's parents were Indian and had four other children in addition to their only daughter. It soon became clear that none of the family approved of our relationship, which shocked me. I thought any parent would be thrilled to know their daughter was dating a man who was studying to become a doctor. Nobody was impressed. In fact, as we waited for supper to be served, it was like I was invisible to the family. They were all rather upset that I was a white male, and they tore apart my appearance, my attire, my vehicle—basically everything about me— as I twiddled my thumbs. My girlfriend couldn't even comfort me because her parents would not allow us to sit near one another.

Supper was served, and my eyes were watering just from inhaling the spices in this Kolhapuri chicken. I had never sampled an Indian dish, but it looked delicious. I took a large bite and could have died from how spicy it was. I didn't want to seem rude, though, so I swallowed and gulped my entire glass of water. Her family snickered. Because her mother kept making comments about how hard she'd worked on the meal, I felt I needed to finish as much of my plate as I could. I didn't want to offend anyone. I was sweating profusely by the time half my food was gone. I couldn't even take off my dinner jacket because I was sweating so much that I was sure my blouse was soaked, and it wouldn't leave a good impression to present myself to my future in-laws that way.

Just as my girlfriend's mother said something about clearing the table for dessert, I felt my stomach rumble and excused myself to the restroom, where I had the most disgusting and painful bowel movement of my entire life.

I wiped and flushed the toilet blindly. I then removed my dinner jacket and fanned at the wet sweat pools on my blouse. I could almost see through the shirt because it was so damp from sweat. I gave myself a quick sniff test & decided I didn't smell as fresh as I'd hoped, so I removed my blouse and began splashing water on my armpits.

As I was doing this, I just happened to look over and see that the toilet was overflowing. Naturally, I panicked and searched high and low for a toilet plunger. When I couldn't find one, I searched for a toilet wand or anything I could use to possibly clear the clog.

Being a teenager and a panicked one at that, I removed my loafers, socks, and slacks, and I jammed my right foot as far into the toilet as it would go. To this day, I still have absolutely no idea what would compel me to do such a thing, but it worked. As I began to pull my foot out of the canal, the water started to drain.

I heard my girlfriend call my name, and I scrambled to get dressed. My foot was still in the toilet, so when I hurried to move, I fell and felt my ankle snap. I'd never broken a bone before, so I was in a state of shock. After a few seconds, however, I squealed like a pig.

There was a knock on the bathroom door that soon became a furious pounding accompanied by the jiggling of the handle. After about a minute, the door flew open and my girlfriend's father was standing in the doorway with a butter knife in his hand. His expression was one of confusion, as he stood there and stared at the scrawny almost-naked kid on the bathroom floor that was covered in water.

My girlfriend's mother didn't think it was appropriate to allow her daughter to see me that way, so as my girlfriend's brother called for help, the parents stood in the bathroom and complained about how stupid I was and how I ruined their restroom.

When the paramedics came, I asked them to grab my clothes. One of the medics snatched my slacks from the floor and the engagement ring fell out of my pocket. I was on a stretcher and had no way of trying to grab it before anyone could see it, so my girlfriend's mother noticed it, picked it up off the floor, and she started screaming in Marathi. I couldn't understand a single word of what she was saying, but I'd reckon it went something like, "Kill him!" because my girlfriend's father grabbed a wet towel from the towel rack, wound it up like you do when you're going to 'crack the whip' on someone, and he started beating me with the towel. I begged the medics to get me out of there.

My fracture required the insertion of bone plates and screws. The recovery time was estimated to be approximately 12 weeks, but I experienced complications and was admitted again for an infection. I had to postpone med school, and I think I was only allowed to do that because my grandparents knew the Dean and made a considerably large donation to the program.

Despite making a fool out of myself, I convinced my girlfriend to marry me. Unfortunately (or fortunately, depending how you look at it), we realized a week before our nuptials that our differences outweighed our similarities, and we called off the wedding. Our friends and families were thrilled. In fact, my mother's exact words once I broke the news to her were, "Oh, thank God."

The more I think about it, we probably wouldn't have been married long, anyway. Her parents hated me so much that they would have thrown rocks instead of rice, and I'd be dead before we even drove away with our tin cans knocking from the back of my beater.

It's been 40+ years since this happened, but I've managed to remain good friends with my ex. We were present at each other's weddings (to the right people), and we still get a laugh out of explaining why I still walk with a limp and have scars.

-J.R., M.D.
California

Playing Chicken

I was returning a wheelchair to the corral when a woman waddled into the ED lobby. She was in visible pain, and it was obvious she had been crying.

"Ma'am," I asked, "would you like to sit in this?"

She shook her head and told me, "I can't. It hurts to sit."

Because I was triage, there was no reason to return to the back with my next patient going to the desk, so I waited in the triage area and passed time by wiping down my station with Sani-Cloths.

"Jane," the registration girl called in an uneasy stammer.

"One second," I replied.

"Jane!"

I hurried out to the registration desk to find the patient lying on the floor. She was sobbing and breathing heavily.

"It hurts," she cried. "It hurts so bad."

"What hurts?" I asked.

"Please," she begged, "just get it out of me."

I rushed over for a wheelchair and tried to help the patient up, but I couldn't lift her on my own and she was doing little to help.

"Let's get you in this chair," I said to her. "Then we'll take you to a bed and get the rest of your information there."

"Please," cried the patient. "I can't sit. It hurts so bad."

"Call to the back," I told the registration girl. "Tell them I need some help."

Two of my coworkers rolled a bed into the lobby. We carefully lifted the patient onto the bed. She winced and gasped as we moved her, and once she was on the bed she squirmed incessantly.

"What's wrong with her?" one of my coworkers asked me.

I shrugged. "We couldn't get that far."

We wheeled the patient into a room and asked again what hurt.

"I don't even know why I did it," she sobbed. "But now it won't come out."

Those few words gave us an idea of what we were in for, but I was not expecting her reply to my coworker asking, "What won't come out?"

"It's a little chicken," the patient blurted out, before rolling on her side and groaning.

I gave one of my coworkers 'the look,' and I asked the patient, "Did you place something inside yourself?"

"Uh-huh," she sobbed. "Please, I need you to get it out. It hurts."

The patient then leaned over the siderail and vomited.

We helped the patient disrobe and assisted her in dressing in a gown. She vomited twice more.

"We'll get the doctor in here right away," my coworker assured the patient.

"I want a woman," the patient said in a panic. "I don't want a man seeing me like this."

"We can certainly page a female doctor," I said. "But we have to wait a few minutes longer for someone to come from another department."

"Just give me the man then," the patient cried. "I don't care anymore. Please, just get this thing out of me."

Someone peeked in the room and told me that I had a patient waiting out front. I assured the patient that our team would take great care of her, but she pleaded with me to stay. One of my coworkers offered to take my place in triage until the patient was calm enough to be on her own.

Our doctor came in and introduced himself.

"I've been told you have a chicken in one of your cavities?" Doctor Smith asked, as if he had been misinformed.

"Yes," the patient sobbed. "I need you to get it out."

An expression came across the doctor's face that I'd never seen on him before. It was almost an expression of 'gotta see it to believe it.' He grabbed a head lamp from a supply cart in the corner of the room. He wheeled his stool to the end of the patient's bed and asked her to open her legs. She screamed bloody murder. If I hadn't known any better, I would have guessed the woman was in labor or was severely injured.

Doctor Smith lifted the thin sheet covering the patient's lower extremities and folded it back and over her knees. The patient gripped my hand so tightly that I wanted to pull away, but I couldn't because that's how strong she was holding on.

"Huh," the doctor commented. "Well…"

"Get it out," the patient cried. "Please. It hurts so bad."

"Jane, come down here for a second," the doctor beckoned.

He grabbed a pair of gloves and handed them to me as he inspected the patient's vagina.

My eyes popped open as wide as they've ever been when I saw what he saw. The patient was indeed carrying poultry in her vaginal cavity, and furthermore, it closely resembled crowning during labor. She was experiencing light vaginal bleeding, and it looked like she had a bit of tearing already.

"Hurry," the patient cried.

The doctor outlined the opening by hovering his index finger and said to me, "You have smaller hands than I do. Let's see if you can't get in there on the sides and try to yank this sucker out of there."

I assure you, I did try. I couldn't get a single finger in there, and even as I tried, the patient screamed out in pain.

"Jane," said the doctor, "let's get this patient started on Toradol."

I took the doctor's orders and administered the medication. Up until the time it kicked in, the patient was intermittently screaming out in pain. She still cried once we administered the drug, but not nearly as much as before. She was still breathing in hisses and wheezes.

"I want you to try something," the doctor said to the patient.

"I'll do anything," she screamed. "Get it out."

"Have you ever given birth?" the doctor asked.

"No," the patient replied.

"I'm going to have you push," explained the doctor. "I want you to use your Kegel muscles, okay?"

"My what?" the patient asked.

The doctor was flustered and looked to me for help.

"You're going to push like you're trying to squeeze out one last drop of pee," I said to her. "Let's not push like you need to have a bowel movement. Just push like you have to urgently pee."

The patient went through the motions a few times, but all that did was upset her more and leave her breathless. Doctor Smith then tried forceps, but he couldn't get them inserted into the patient's vagina.

We brought X-ray down to the patient's room with their mobile imaging device and were able to see that the patient indeed had a raw Cornish hen in her vaginal cavity. The bird had turned sideways, and a wing was visibly dislocated. There was no way I could see her 'birthing' the hen. It was a few inches wider than a newborn's head. I know the human body can be pushed to amazing limits, but I don't think she would have been able to do this on her own, not the way the bird had shifted inside her.

Doctor Smith called up to OB and requested an OB-GYN for an emergency episiotomy. The patient was prepped with a local anesthetic and the episiotomy was performed.

We removed a 2.2-pound Cornish hen from the patient's vagina. She could not drive home following her visit, so she called a female friend to pick her up. I never did hear her tell her friend why she was in the ED.

The patient never explained to us why she inserted the hen in her vagina, nor did she explain **how** she got it in there. She was the talk of the ED all night and for some time after. I think about this often and have absolutely no idea what would possess someone to do something so absurd, nor do I understand how she even got the thing shoved up there in the first place. I have so many unanswered questions.

This is a case of 'you had to be there' to fully appreciate the shock and total bewilderment of our ED staff that night. I've heard some stories in my life, but I'd never seen anything quite like this.

-J.R.-S.

Location withheld at request

(Author's note: I have no words. This is right up there with that nutcracker story from 'Tis the Season.)

Tooth and Nail

My first day on the job as ED Security was eventful. I don't know what started the fight, but I put an end to it.

Two senior citizen men were throwing punches (weak punches, but punches nonetheless) and rolling around on the floor. One of the nurses said they were fighting over a pair of dentures.

I didn't believe her until my partner and I got the men pulled apart, but lo and behold, there were a pair of false teeth on the hallway floor.

No charges were filed. We simply placed the men in their respective treatment rooms and monitored the rooms in case they tried to scrap again. I don't know what happened to the teeth.

-G.G.

New Hampshire

Growing Old Doesn't Mean You Have to Grow Up

I was floating on the hospice floor one night and thought it was a breeze. Most of our patients were comfortably sedated or were asleep. It was easy money. Someone from the previous shift had left pizza behind, too, so that was a bonus.

After a few hours, I received a call from an irate male. He stated someone had called him from my phone number, and he demanded answers. Since he'd been woken out of a dead sleep in the middle of the night, I certainly understood why he was so upset. I apologetically explained that when someone receives a call from the hospital with our floor extension, that just means anyone on the floor could have placed that call. It rings back to our station, but the callback number is just a blanket number. Since we shared a large floor with rehab, it could have been any patient, family member, or staff member placing the calls. There was no way to determine who placed the calls or really stop someone from placing calls.

Thankfully, the caller seemed satisfied with this explanation and worriedly wondered aloud if a friend or family member was admitted to the hospital.

A few minutes later I received a call from a 911 dispatcher. Before he could realize that I was just a nurse on the floor, he sternly informed me that what I was doing was illegal and if it happened again he would send officers to my location.

"Sir," I replied, "this is a blanket number for two hospital units. I don't even know what you're talking about. I'm a registered nurse on Hospice."

The dispatcher then explained that he'd received three prank calls from someone at our phone number.

"How do you know they were pranks?" I remember asking him.

"Because she keeps calling and asking me what's for lunch and saying weird things."

I assured the dispatcher that I would do rounds and check on my patients and their families, as well as check the phone in the commons area. I stated I would also call down to rehab and let the nurses know so they could do rounds.

All was well until I came to my next-to-last patient. Jane was approximately 90-years-old and was in end-stage of her diagnosis. Doctors did not expect her to live until Christmas, which was only a few weeks away.

I found Jane curled up in her bed, with the phone resting on her legs. She slammed down the headset and giggled uncontrollably with her roommate, a woman in her 70s.

"Are you ladies causing trouble?" I asked.

Jane waved me off and said, "Just a few harmless giggles."

Jane had been making prank calls to every number listed in the hospital directory she'd found in her night stand, from other departments to local pharmacies.

While I was still present in the room, Jane said excitedly to her roommate, "We should call Dominos and ask them for Pizza Hut's number."

"Jane, why are you doing this?" I asked.

She laughed and said, "I'm dying, honey, but I'm not dead yet. I have a little more living to do."

I explained to Jane that I couldn't stop her from making prank calls (nor did I really see the harm in it), but I did request that she not call 911 again.

I also learned that the pizza left by the previous shift was Jane's doing. She had called a pizza place and ordered five large pizzas to Hospice. When the delivery girl arrived, the nurses were surprised and said they didn't order pizza, but they pooled together with rehab, pharmacy, and ER to pay for the pizzas, so each department could take one.

"Well I won't tell them you were behind it," I promised Jane.

Jane giggled and said, "I don't care if you tell them or not. What are they gonna do, arrest me?"

Jane passed away a few days later, so I'm glad she got to spend her last days enjoying herself. It was truly like I had walked in on pre-teens having a sleepover, and I can't remember the last time I had that much carefree fun.

-T.O.-J.
Delaware

It was Christmas Eve and we hadn't had a single patient all night. I crossed my legs under myself in my chair, and I put my head down on my desk. I fell asleep that way, while my coworkers did the same or browsed the internet.

I guess I jerked or something, because my chair swiveled, and I fell out of it. A few people saw and were laughing, so I tried to get up and brush it off.

My foot was asleep, so when I put weight on it, I collapsed and fell again. I didn't even feel the pain until my foot started waking up.

I sprained my ankle and had to use crutches for a while.

-K.T.

Oklahoma

People Say the Darnedest Things

Readers share some outrageous things they've heard from patients, prisoners, family members, or coworkers.

■■■

My patient was a frat boy in his early 20s. He presented with a chief complaint of constipation and stated he hadn't had a bowel movement in nearly two weeks.

"Have you ever had an enema before?" I asked.

He looked at me like I'd just told him I came from Mars and said with a shake of his head, "No, I'm friends with everyone."

-B.K., M.D.

Florida

■■■

Way back when, I worked at a scummy SNF. And I'm being literal when I tell you the only reason I stayed so long is that I was scared for my residents. (Luckily, the facility and its supervisors were eventually investigated, shut down, and its residents were moved to a much cleaner, safer environment).

My favorite patient was 102-years-old and it didn't matter what was occurring around him, he was always the kindest, most jovial person you could meet. One time, the sprinkler system went berserk and this man laid in his bed for 30 minutes before one of the facility's managers even realized one of the sprinklers was malfunctioning. He shrugged it off when anyone else would find themselves seething.

One time, when I was having a particularly rough day, I sighed and asked him, "What's your secret? You're never frustrated about anything."

I thought he'd give some lecture about how life is short and meant to be cherished— you know, I was waiting for some inspirational quote I could paint on a canvas and hang next to my key rack to see every morning as I left the house.

My patient shrugged and said, "I can't be mad because I can't remember half of what happens to me."

-L.G.

Indiana
■■

While arresting my subject for attempting to buy cocaine from an undercover officer, he angrily declared, "It's not illegal if a cop is selling it. Maybe someone should arrest you for selling it to all these people on the streets and getting all these people [effed] up."

I tried to explain to him that wasn't *exactly* how it worked, but he wasn't having it.

-S.R.

Ohio
■■

I was paged to speak to one of our ESD patients, as he had requested to speak with a House Supervisor.

As a little bit of a background, this patient had blindfolded himself and jumped out of a 15-foot tree while his friend filmed it for social media.

When I entered the room, I was expecting the patient to complain about his care or complain that we weren't giving him enough Dilaudid.

Instead, he demanded to know if he could sue the city. His reason? "That sidewalk was way too hard. Concrete's not supposed to be that hard, man."

The patient had multiple fractures and was found in illegal possession of a firearm and narcotics, so I'm pretty sure he had bigger fish to fry, but whatever. He wasn't satisfied when I couldn't answer his question and informed him I had no time to stand around and answer stupid questions, so he threw a fit and had to eventually be restrained.

-K.W.

New Jersey

One day I was working, and a patient came in without parental supervision. The kid was about 17 and was teary-eyed. He stated he had a private concern and refused to divulge more to registration clerks or our manager. We all started thinking that maybe the kid was being abused or something, so we notified the Charge Nurse, and she told us to go ahead and sign the kid in. She said if they needed to call CPS they would, but if it happened to be a less serious issue they'd explain it to the kid and then call his parents. No big deal.

All this hype, and you know what I heard him say as I was walking to the bathroom?

"My mom just said my brother has hemorrhoids, and I need to know if I have them too. Sometimes we drink out of the same Gatorade bottle, and yesterday I slept with his girlfriend."

-J.S.

Illinois

My patient had been transferred from prison for several minor ailments. Despite the fact that he was well-known in our community as a child molester, I offered him the best care possible.

Unfortunately, I couldn't offer him the care he felt he was entitled to. Believe me, this man treated our ED like it was the Hilton or something, and every five seconds he was demanding something else from me. It became so bad that I had to pull someone from another department to answer his call light because our department was hectic, and I just didn't have time to remake my patient's tea because the water was half-a-degree too cold or hot, especially when I was dealing with patients with more critical injuries and/or illnesses.

The woman I'd put in charge of answering the gentleman's call light rushed over to me. I told Pharmacy I'd have to call them back.

"What happened?" I asked.

The woman was pale and looked dizzy, so I made her sit down. Her hands were shaking as she said frantically, "He wanted a blanket, so I was going to get him one. But then he wanted another glass of water, so I went to get that first because someone else wanted water.

Well, I took the guy his water, and he pulled his catheter out right in front of me. The balloon and everything!"

When I entered the room and confronted the patient about his behavior, he laughed and said, "Don't need a warm blanket if you have warm piss."

He seemed to pride himself in the fact that we had to change his bedding. He was pissed off when Attending ordered us to fit the patient with an adult diaper.

-O.T.

Colorado
■■■■■■■■■■■■■■■■■■■■■■■■■■■■■■■■■■■■■■■

My patient's phone rang just as I stepped in the room. She laughed and said, "These kids are gonna be the death of me."

Her husband elbowed me in the ribs and whispered, "I hope it's soon. It'll be easier than telling her I want a divorce."

-T.E.

Pennsylvania
■■■■■■■■■■■■■■■■■■■■■■■■■■■■■■■■■■■■■■■

We were staging at the circus one year, and since we had some time to kill before the performance, we opened our ambulance for the kids to explore. Most of the kids were mesmerized by all the buttons and equipment, and we flipped on the lights and sirens a few times.

Most of the comments we heard were what you'd expect to hear from kids ranging from 2-years-old to 14-years-old. You know, the kids wanted to help people or wanted to drive a vehicle that had sirens, things like that.

This one girl, who'd very proudly informed us that she was four, said loudly, "This is what I'm gonna drive when I grow up. I can't wait to be able to call people idiots and do this." She then stuck up her middle finger and waved it around like she was just cut off in traffic.

To be honest, I'd really like to be able to do that, too. I'm sure I'd be fired in about two seconds if I ever dared to follow through, but a man can dream.

"You are *not* riding with your grandpa anymore," said her embarrassed mother.

"Grandpa doesn't do that," the child tattled. "Nana does."

-W.V.

Virginia
■■■

My brother is handicapable. He is wheelchair bound and has the mental capacity of a young child. When I was younger I used to be embarrassed to be seen in public with my brother because he often throws temper tantrums or say things you would think are inappropriate for someone his physical age to say.

Earlier that day, my brother heard a newscaster mention a story about rape. He asked my mom what it meant. She tried to explain the best she could in a way that he could understand it, but part of her also wanted to keep him sheltered from the world, which is how he's physically in his late-20s and still thinks that babies come from a stork. My mom's explanation was, "Rape is when

54

someone makes you do something you don't want to do."

This definition must have stuck in his head, because my brother announced loudly to the entire waiting room, "My sister raped me before we came here."

He was referring to how before his appointment we had gone grocery shopping and when we returned home to drop off the groceries, I made him brush his teeth. I only made him brush after discovering that he'd found a bag of Starbursts in the backseat of my car and ate 16 of them (from what I could tell by the wrappers) while I was driving.

Because we were in an office that primarily dealt with other handicapable patients, someone felt it necessary to report my brother's comments to a staff member, and we were briefly investigated by adult social services. The caseworker was laughing so hard once we explained the situation.

-T.R.
Arizona
■■■

My three-year-old son and I accompanied my wife to a doctor's appointment following mandatory labs for her dizziness. The N.P. entered the room and congratulated my wife on her pregnancy. We were shocked because we were using contraceptives and never considered pregnancy a reason for my wife's dizzy spells.

"Mommy's having a baby because she put my daddy's wee-wee in her mouth," my son beamed to the N.P.

He said this just as the N.P. was sitting on her stool, and she was so flabbergasted that she missed the seat and fell to the floor.

We were mortified that our child would rat us out after walking in on us the night before. We had to have a long talk with him because the next day he told his daycare teacher the same thing.

-Initials and location withheld at request

Idiot

During an overnight shift, we received a walk-in for a chief complaint of narcoticsitis, which is a condition more commonly known in the medical profession as 'drug seeking.'

The entire time the patient was admitted to the ER, he was belligerent and violent. When he learned he was not getting narcotics, he assaulted a pregnant nurse and stormed out of the ER. On his way out of the hospital, he'd managed to swipe a prescription pad that our doctor had been using. (Under normal circumstances our doctor wouldn't have left the pad lying around, but he was in the middle of writing a script when we received a walk-in pediatric code.)

We called the police and kept an eye on the patient, hoping to be able to catch a vehicle description, license plate number, or hopefully be able to point the responding officers in the right direction if the patient left.

The patient wandered the parking lot for a few minutes and finally pulled out his phone. We were all confused.

A second set of police officers arrived at our ER parking lot. The first officers were responding to our call to report the patient for assault and theft. Want to know why the second set of officers showed up?

The patient called 911 to report that his car had been stolen from the ER parking lot.

As the patient was being arrested, he spied his car two rows over. Nobody stole it; he'd just forgotten where he parked.

The funny thing about this is that it was determined the patient used false information and was driving a stolen vehicle. If he had only remembered where he parked, he probably would have gotten away with it all.

-P.Y.

South Carolina

<u>Last Resort</u>

I think sometimes people look at nurses and think we're all snooty or something just because we have a no-nonsense demeanor after dealing with crude and rude patients all day. Let me tell you, though, I am just like everyone else, and I have all the same problems everyone else has. In fact, I think I may have some more severe problems from time to time.

I'm a little embarrassed to say that my daughter was a problematic child. Her father found 'love' in a 19-year-old Hooters waitress and left us during my daughter's pre-teen years. Five weeks earlier, I had given birth to twins (one of my sons has Downs), so as a single mother with two babies—one special needs— on the boob non-stop and as a nurse who worked 70+ hours a week, I don't think I was capable of giving my daughter the attention she so desperately needed.

I don't know if this is how it worked for other parents with problematic children, but once my daughter started spiraling out of control, I didn't feel like there was much I could do to stop it. When I learned she was into drugs and alcohol at age 13, I tried to lock down the house. Unfortunately, while I was at work, she sneaked away from the house and the babysitter had no idea. My daughter was found two days later, three counties away.

Truly, I was devastated at what type of young woman my daughter was growing to be. When I thought about her future, all I could picture was her in jail or worse. I work in ES and see addicts day in and day out. I treat women for domestic violence injuries. I speak to addict prostitutes who come in and test positive for every STD known to man. I never thought my daughter would be headed down that road.

After my daughter said something about wanting to have a baby, I dragged my her to a gynecologist and tried to get her put on the pill. But, I was informed that if my daughter didn't want to be on birth control, there was very little I could do. The gyno reminded me that even if my daughter used birth control, it would still be possible to become infected with a sexual transmitted disease. I left the office in tears, and my daughter walked out of there like she'd just won a war.

That very night, my daughter sneaked out of her bedroom window and was brought home by two police officers. She had been found having sex with a boy behind a dumpster, and she was so drunk that she couldn't stand up.

Social services became involved, and no matter what anyone suggested or what advice parenting magazines or internet groups for moms had…I couldn't control my daughter. She got worse as the year progressed. I slapped her once (she called me a bad name and said my husband left because I made 'retarded' babies). After I hit her, she called the police on me. Thankfully, the responding officer was familiar with our problems and told my daughter she needed to straighten up.

My daughter was completely out of control and was hellbent on breaking all the rules. She became fixated with this plan to become pregnant and told me daily that when she had her baby, she wouldn't fail as a mother like I did. It was so painful to hear those words from a 14-year-old.

I was at work one night and had a panic attack when a teenage mother came in for a labor check. It was so bad that Charge sent me home and suggested I visit the hospital's counseling department. I felt like everyone was watching and judging me for being a failure of a parent. Even more, when I thought of how stuck I felt and how out of control our situation was, I couldn't breathe.

When I came home that night, I found my daughter having sex on the balcony just off the upstairs guest room. The boy ran off before I could catch and kill him. I couldn't even yell at my daughter anymore. I just sighed and told her to go to bed, and then I used the money I planned to pay the cable bill with to keep the sitter overnight.

I tried to sleep, but I couldn't. It was nothing new. I hadn't really slept in more than a year. I think my body had adapted to sleeping two hours a night. I couldn't stop thinking about how the bills were piling up or how the law couldn't seem to find my husband to serve divorce papers or get child support or even get his name off the mortgage so that I could try to refinance under my own name and income bracket. I thought about my sons' futures and how I would be able to give them the attention they needed. My heart palpitated when I thought about my daughter. I honestly felt like I was having a heart attack. And I know it's a horrible thing to say because I love all my kids to death and also did at that time, but part of me was hoping the chest pains were the real deal. Maybe I was a failure, and maybe my kids were going to be better off without me. I don't even remember falling asleep, but I woke up a few hours later.

When I went downstairs, my sitter was in the living room with my twins. They were eating cut up bananas off a plate and she was watching some movie on TV. Of course, because the universe wanted to throw my situation back in my face, it was a movie about a woman giving birth.

Apparently, there was a very graphic scene where the camera panned to the actress's pelvic area and showed the baby crowning. My sitter became disgusted and dry heaved. She quickly turned the channel.

A lightbulb went off above my head.

With the help of the internet and some of my coworkers from ES and OB, we found exactly what I was looking for.

I sent the twins to my sister's house that night, and I called my daughter downstairs. She smelled like marijuana, but I ignored that. Naturally, she gave me attitude, but I told her to sit down and get through 30 minutes of TV time with me, and then I would stay out of her life forever if she wanted me to.

We watched video after video of women giving birth, from the screaming, tearing, pooping on the table, leaning over and puking during a hard push…You name it. If it's ever occurred during labor, I made my daughter watch it. For good measure, I included a few scenes from C-Sections, both during the procedure and also of the scars afterward. She tried to get off the couch a few times, but I told her if she left the room I was going to send her to boarding school. I don't think she knew that I couldn't pay for that, so she sat there with her arms crossed and made groaning noises the entire time.

After the birthing videos, I showed my daughter a slide show of sexually transmitted diseases.

Our 30 minutes was up, and I told my daughter she could go. She began to stomp off to her room when I stopped her, pointed to the pack and play in the corner, and said, "By the way, that thing cost sixty dollars. Diapers for the boys are almost two hundred a month. Think about it, Jane."

I wish I could say that solved all my problems, but it didn't. It *did*, however, stop my daughter from being reckless with her body and these outlandish fantasies of becoming a mother at 14. She still sneaked out of the house and she still got in trouble at school, but from all the poking and prodding I did, she wasn't having sex anymore, at least as far as I could tell.

I finally tracked down my husband and he signed the divorce papers. We lost the house in a foreclosure and we to move to another state to live in my parents' basement for a while. Things were rough, but that seemed to knock some sense into my daughter and her behavior changed radically.

I met a man a few months after we moved to Oregon, and we married shortly after. He has a special needs daughter and a story similar to mine, minus the crazy problem child teen.

By the way, my daughter is now 19 and still hasn't become pregnant. She is completely sober now and is attending college to become a child psychologist. One weekend she came home to do laundry, hugged me out of the blue, and told me she was sorry for how she acted when she was younger. That made it all worth it.

-P.G.

Oregon

A real chief complaint sent in by O.R. of Indiana:

"An owl broke in my third-story apartment at two in the morning, bit me, and then stole all my Percocet. Now you have to give me a refill because it's the law."

<u>Misspelling?</u>

Something went screwy with our software, so while I.T. was working on the network, we had to do everything by hand, including registration and charting. To make this somewhat easier on the registration staff, we gave them forms for patients to complete. The top portions of the forms would contain the patients' contact information, while the bottom portion of the forms would have a blank area for the patients' complaints. Patients would write in their ailments/age/rate their pain, and then return the form to the desk, where registration would remove the bottom portion of the form for our triage nurse to place on a pegboard.

I was triaging that night, and I was arranging my pegboard complaints by severity. Runny noses could wait. Chest pains could not.

As I continued to go through the pieces of paper, I noticed a particularly concerning chief complaint: "Got stepped on by whores!!!!"

I started laughing and couldn't stop. I knew what the patient meant, but my brain saw the unfortunate misspelling and rolled with it. I'm sure this patient wasn't the first in the world to misspell 'horse,' but I'd never seen it spelled *that* way.

Wanting to get the patient checked out for internal injuries, I called him to the triage room. He walked slowly and hissed with each step he took. His face was beat up pretty badly, too.

As he sat down, I asked him, "So how big was the horse?"

He looked confused and asked, "Huh?"

I motioned to his complaint form that I held in my hand. "Says here you got stepped on by a horse."

He shook his head and said angrily, "No, WHORES. I got in a fight with a woman outside of a bar, and all her friends started kicking the shit out of me."

The patient lifted his shirt and his chest was black and blue from bruising. He even had a puncture wound from what appeared to be a stiletto shoe.

I think this caught me off guard more than when I had thought the patient misspelled 'horse,' because instead of laughing, all I could do was stammer. The patient requested that we call the police to report the incident.

Just when I thought the night couldn't get any weirder, about an hour after we discharged that patient, officers brought in two jail clearances. The patients were drag queens, dressed in sparkly sequin dresses that left very little to the imagination, as well as wore heels that were at least seven-inches, making them tower over everyone else because the patients were already a good six-feet-tall.

I got nosy and asked why they were going to jail, when an officer told me, "Remember that guy we interviewed a little bit ago? These are the ladies that beat him up."

Wild night.

-A.P.
New Jersey

<u>Misunderstanding</u>

My first appointment of the day was a 40-year-old woman whose religion prevented her from using contraceptives for family planning. As a result of this, my patient had recently given birth to her twelfth child since having her first at the age of 17. I am not sure what caused the woman and her husband to seek my advice after that particular number of children, but she and her husband were in my office at 8 a.m. to discuss options to prevent future pregnancies.

The couple seemed fearful to even be at the appointment, first of all. They repeatedly cited their religion and told me they were afraid that someone from the church would discover that they'd even attended a consultation with my practice. Both parties tearfully explained how they were faithful to their religious beliefs, but the wife sobbed, "I don't know how it feels to not be pregnant and know that I'm going to be pregnant again in a few months."

It was certainly not my place to judge the couples' religious beliefs, but my heart broke for that poor woman as she told me that she and her husband always imagined having 'maybe five or six' children. They were surprised by two sets of twins over the course of years, in addition to their other children. The husband let out an awkward laugh and stated he had no idea the couple would be so fertile. They came to me in secrecy and wanted to learn about permanent sterilization procedures, and hopefully one that was 'not noticeable' to their congregation.

We worked together to learn about tubal ligation and its recovery time. Based on the wife's medical background, however, we determined that she may have been at risk for complications following the procedure. She cried.

"Another option is a vasectomy," I suggested.

I proceeded to explain how the procedure was much simpler in terms of privacy, recovery time, and complications.

The husband became irate, and I was unsure as to why. He began saying what I like to call 'church curses.' I first heard of these curses from my great-grandmother, a devout Baptist. If she ever lost her temper and started mumbling under her breath, "Jiminy Cricket," or, "Holy Betsy," you'd do best to get out of her way.

The patient's husband was spouting off so many more creative cursing alternatives than my great-grandmother ever did. He then stood up and knocked some papers off my desk, all while telling me I was crazy.

"No siree, Bob," he yelled. "No sir. I am not letting you chop off my penis."

He then stormed out of the room and slammed my office door so hard that a frame holding my credentials fell off the wall.

I was beside myself and could only choke out, "Does your husband think a vasectomy is an appendage removal?"

She seemed surprised and asked, "Isn't it?"

I hurriedly explained the procedure to my patient and she simply stated, "Oh," before telling me she would go find her husband and explain the procedure to him.

A few minutes later, the couple returned to my office and the husband apologized for his outburst. He actually laughed, embarrassed, and said, "Sorry, sir. I thought you wanted to amputate my member. Can't let you do that. I've grown quite fond of the fella."

I shrugged it off and told him I could certainly understand how the thought of losing my manhood would cause me upset.

The couple asked if they could take some time to weigh their options, and that was fine with me, so they left, and I continued with my scheduled appointments.

A week later, the couple returned to my office and stated they decided upon a vasectomy because—get this—the wife was pregnant five weeks after giving birth. It was an emotional appointment because the two were obviously not happy with knowing they were having another child. It sort of became a therapy session because they told me they couldn't tell anyone about their true feelings and 'had to let it out.'

I know that as a physician I am not supposed to get emotionally involved with patients or their predicaments, but my heart truly hurt for this couple, and I wanted to do everything possible to assist them.

We performed the procedure the next day and the two were ecstatic afterward. I don't know what happened to them after they left my office, but I wish them well.

-C.G., M.D.

Pennsylvania

Wash Your Sins Away

For my first call of the evening, I responded to a call regarding a domestic violence complaint. When I arrived on scene, I found a badly-beaten female lying unconscious, half in and half out of the entryway to her home. She was in bad shape and appeared to have been stabbed in the abdomen and taken a blow to the back of the head by a heavy object. What's worse is that her toddler was trying to wake his mother up, and the baby was covered in his mother's blood.

After calling EMS and clearing the scene, I arrested a 92-year-old woman for pepper spraying a cashier for counting back her change incorrectly.

After that, I was one of six officers responding to a massive brawl across town. Apparently, a local drug dealer was afraid the 'pigs' were watching his drug den, so he began dealing out of his neighbors' yards and caused a bloody fight that involved seven adult men and women.

That's the kind of day I was having. I felt bad for feeling so frustrated, just because I knew that instead I should have felt grateful that it wasn't myself in those situations. It's difficult, however, to deal with the insanity of the job sometimes. When I enlisted in the academy, I always envisioned myself writing traffic tickets or responding to noise complaints. I didn't know that every shift would be a CrossFit workout or that I would end up in the emergency room 12 times in my first year and a half for job-related injuries.

With 10 minutes left on the clock before I could go to the station and begin my end-of-shift routine, dispatch radioed and stated I was the nearest officer to a report of a sighting of a violent offender. The subject is question was wanted for a slew of violent crimes, robberies, and possession of firearms and drugs, as well as dealing drugs.

Honestly, I wasn't in the mood to deal with this type of situation. I wanted to turn around and drive 900 miles in the opposite direction.

When I arrived at the residence, the subject yelled at the homeowner, "John, I can't believe your bitch-ass would call the cops on me."

Of course, the subject then ran. I chased him on foot for what felt like an eternity. He was young, agile, and obviously physically fit. That was all evident, as the subject leapt over hoods of vehicles, dashed through yards, and cleared fences.

After three blocks, I finally closed in on the subject and ordered him to the ground. Realizing he was literally trapped between an officer and a brick wall, the subject complied.

As I was cuffing him, the subject started protesting. "Man, you can't arrest me," he said.

"I can, and I am," I replied.

"But I was dissolved of my sins," he told me.

"Absolved?" I laughed.

"Man, whatever," he said. "My friend Jane told me to go on down to the church and so I did. They dunked me in water and said I'm clean now."

"Uh-huh," I said, trying to hide that my heart felt like it was beating out of my chest.

"So you can't arrest me because God forgave me of my sins."

"Well the police department didn't," I told him.

He groaned and said, "That's some real bullshit, man. Jesus doesn't care that I stole a Camaro."

Vehicular theft had not been on the subject's list of charges, but he kept talking and waived his right to an attorney, so we were able to connect him to a series of auto thefts from the weekend prior.

-K.E.

Illinois

Wow!

My appendectomy was performed by a surgeon whom I had a secret crush on. We worked together frequently, so I thought it was best that I never say anything.

The night before my surgery, my coworker confided in me that the surgeon took her home for a one-night stand and he threw her out of his apartment within seconds of finishing the deed. She stated the sex was bad, anyway, thanks to the surgeon's premature ejaculation and small penis. This nurse also informed me that the surgeon had slept with almost every nurse on our floor except me.

Obviously, my opinion of the man changed, but I'm professional and can separate work from my personal life.

At least I can when I'm not coming out of surgery.

My sister has a cell phone video of me telling my surgeon, "You know what, buster? I think you're really hot, but I heard you're a bad person with a tiny penis. But I still think you're hot, and that's probably why I'm 30 and still single, because I'm obviously stupid."

I then started sobbing and asked, "You can have sex with Jane, but all you ever do is have break room coffee with me? I have liked you for so long! Oh, God. I'm gonna die alone."

When I came down from the drugs, I only knew I had said those things because my sister insisted upon showing me the video repeatedly. She thought it was the funniest thing she'd ever seen. I, on the other hand, was mortified. How could I *ever* face the doctor again? He didn't even come in the room to discharge me. He sent in a nurse with my discharge papers and instructions, and I was told to 'call the floor' if I had any questions or concerns.

I avoided speaking to my coworkers while I was on the mend. I deactivated my Facebook account and refused to acknowledge text messages. My first day back at work was utter chaos.

In a really twisted turn of events, the coworker who'd confided in me was arrested for filing a false police report (among other things), and she was fired from her job. She allegedly told the story she told me about four other physicians within our network, and she was found guilty of spiking one doctor's work drink with the date rape drug. I guess things started to come to light because after I exploded at my surgeon/coworker, he started to dig around and ask everyone why I would say something like that. Everyone started saying that she said she lied because the men rejected her advances. The hospital cleaned out her locker and found a weird shrine to one of the OB doctors, where she had cut out pictures of the doctor and his family from our facility's monthly updates pamphlet. She used a red sharpie to scribble out his wife's face from the pictures. I knew she was a bit eccentric, yeah, but I had no idea I was working with a nutcase. Before finding out about her little shrine, I only thought that kind of stuff happened in movies.

The surgeon I insulted and made a fool out of myself in front of cautiously approached me on my second day of work. I turned beet red and apologized profusely for my behavior (and told him that I don't think I've ever called someone 'buster' before), but he laughed it off. He then said he didn't know that I was attracted to him, but he was thrilled to hear that because he'd wanted to ask me out since we first met but was afraid it would offend me or would cross the line of professionalism.

We actually got married a few months ago, and we just found out we are expecting. I have no clue what happened to my ex-coworker, but I do know that we have strict instructions to call security if she ever sets foot on hospital property again. I just thought I'd share our crazy love story!

-K.I.

Location withheld at request

Personal Results May Vary

I responded to an ICU Code Blue. I ran up three flights of stairs. Three rooms before the code, I tripped over a syringe cap, fell, and heard my knee crack. Still, I hurried to the patient's room to assist.

I had been doing chest compressions for 43-seconds and all I do was hope someone would tag team me out of rotation for a break.

The room was dead silent, except for our team shuffling around. Everyone seemed to have a good grasp on what to do and when.

Out of nowhere, the patient let out a long, loud fart before gasping for air.

He seemed to have no understanding about what had just occurred. He cluelessly asked, "What are y'all doing?"

I couldn't help but to laugh out of relief.

"You almost died," a nurse explained.

The patient, no kidding, looked over at a doctor and said, "No shit?"

Never before and never since have I ever seen a patient respond that way after a code and especially so quickly. I'm telling you, although his vitals were a little wonky, the patient himself was the most alert, unaffected person in the entire room.

I had to go to ES as a workman's comp and it turns out I had a patellar fracture. I was on crutches for seven weeks.

-M.R.
South Carolina

When I was a CNA in an SNF, I had some feisty residents. The resident with the most attitude was Jane, who was 103-years-young. And if you ever used that phrase, she'd call you a slew of names before telling you, "I'm not young, damn it."

One day, I told Jane, "Hey, your sons just called. They said they're coming to visit for Christmas."

"I'll believe it when I see it," she said. "You should call them back and tell them I died," she said with a cough. "Get their hopes up like they do mine."

I didn't know whether to cry or laugh, but I didn't feel like I had very much choice in the matter because Jane slapped my hand and said, "Bitch, that's funny and you know it."

-R.S.
Wisconsin

Didn't Think That Through

I sat down with my patient after it was determined that she needed a colonoscopy. Because most (if not all) of my patients fear the procedure, I try to sit down with them and explain sedation options and go through the procedure beforehand. I usually find this works better than, "Okay, we're going to schedule the procedure," and then the patients will spend the entire drive home imagining the worst.

I said to my patient, "Most patients are concerned with pain when it comes to a colonoscopy."

My patient made eye contact, had a dead serious expression on her face, and she said, "Oh, I'm not worried. My boyfriend and I do anal all the time."

I didn't even think about how my response would sound, so I just laughed and said, "Nice. Lucky."

My patient started laughing as I tried to backpedal and explain that I meant that she was lucky to not worry about the common fears regarding the procedure. The damage was done, though.

Thankfully, the patient was forgiving and understanding. If she hadn't been, I'm sure I would be sitting in front of the Board right now, trying to explain myself and fight to keep my license.

-A.L., M.D.
Colorado

I was wiping after using the restroom, when I felt a terrible pain in my chest. I called 911 because I always heard my nurse friends talking about how chest pain can radiate.

Got to the hospital and had a bunch of tests run, only to find out my rib slipped out of place as I was wiping.

I felt so embarrassed.

-Initials and location withheld at request

<u>People Suck</u>

During a busy shift, we were having to place non-emergent patients in rooms and leave them for periods of time in excess of 15 minutes. We did our best to explain that it would take some time before we could see our non-emergent patients, and though some seemed agitated, most understood.

We had three patients code at the same time. Every last RN, tech, M.D., P.A. rushed to those three rooms. It was truly an all-hands on deck scenario. Our poor Unit Clerk had to pull a receptionist from the ED lobby, which in turn left their department short. It was total chaos.

As my coworker was pumping away at compressions and I was pushing adrenaline, a patient I had seated in a non-trauma bay for a complaint of one stuffy nostril barged in the room and screamed at the top of his lungs, "I told you guys that I CAN'T BREATHE, DAMN IT!"

One of my coworkers served in the military and never seemed a bit fazed by anything. She looked over to him with an annoyed expression and said, "Seems like you're doing a good job to me."

The patient charged at the RN who was doing chest compressions, and he knocked her to the ground.

He screamed, "This lady's practically dead, anyway. Why don't you try to take care of the people that need it?"

So we did. Two other patients heard the ruckus and restrained the man until law enforcement arrived. The man was arrested for striking our RN, but not before he whined that he injured his knee as officers took him down.

As a safety precaution, we performed a quick medical clearance and found the patient's knee was fine, just perhaps a bit bruised.

-K.E.

Washington

Back when I worked as a receptionist at our local hospital, we had just hired a new transporter. His supervisor decided to have a little fun, so he ordered the transporter to go to the supply department and request some items.

The transporter made it to the supply department and said to the clerk, "My boss sent me here for Fallopian tubes."

Of course, everyone cracked up immediately, and once the transporter realized what he'd requested, he was mortified.

Poor guy wouldn't look at anyone for a week!

-M.P.
California

I Need a Room

I temporarily switched from floor RN to ER receptionist for a few weeks, following an incident that left me shaken and unable to concentrate on my RN tasks. (A patient followed me from work to my home and assaulted me.)

My first patient during my short stint as receptionist made my blood boil.

I watched a pretty young girl enter the lobby. She was wearing a sorority sweatshirt and leggings, while carrying a handbag that probably cost more than my car note. She was on her phone, furiously texting.

"UGH!" she screamed.

As a nurse, I've learned to let people come to you. If you ask, "What's the matter?" or, "Are you in pain?" then nine times out of 10 you're going to get an exaggerated response back. So I kept my mouth shut and waited for the girl to come to the desk.

"Sign me in," she demanded.

"I just need to see a photo ID, please," I stated.

She rolled her eyes and then grabbed her driver's license out of a wallet that also probably cost more than my car note. She threw it at me.

I don't stand for that, so I had no problem sternly telling her, "Don't throw anything at me."

She snorted and said snidely, "It was an accident."

I didn't even blink when I said, "Don't let it happen again."

The girl rolled her eyes as I entered her in the system.

"And what brings you here today?" I asked.

"My boyfriend is being a huge douche, so I want a room."

I kind of blankly stared at the girl before saying, "No, I mean why do you need to see a doctor?"

"I just told you."

"Are you sick?" I asked, growing agitated.

"Sick of my boyfriend's crap," she laughed.

"But are you ill?"

She looked confused and said, "Uh, no," in an exaggerated Valley Girl voice.

"If you're not sick," I asked, "then why are you in the emergency room?"

She stomped on the ground and said, "Do you not even listen?"

She raised her voice and looked around as she called out, "Hello? Can I get someone competent?"

"If you're not sick or injured," I said, "then I think we're done here."

"But I need a room."

"This isn't the Sheraton," I replied curtly.

"I told my boyfriend that this was his last chance. I want a room so I can tell him I'm at the hospital and make him feel bad about ignoring me."

"We don't do that here," I said.

"But I want a room."

"No," I said.

She laughed and threw her credit card at me, even though I'd just told her not to throw stuff at me.

"Just ring it up, honey," she demanded. "Charge me twice if you want, I don't care. Just don't even think about telling me no. You have no idea who my mom is."

"I don't care who your mom is," I chuckled angrily. "If you're not sick or injured, you don't need to be here. This is the emergency room, where people come when they're dying so we can save them. This isn't some place to come to get revenge on your boyfriend."

The girl then SPIT on me and told me that her mother was a higher-up at the university and would have my job.

Instead of rolling my eyes (like I very much wanted to do), I smiled sweetly and said, "Oh, I had no idea! Let me get someone better equipped to assist you."

I placed her ID and credit card back on the counter and walked to the back. I phoned security and explained I needed the girl escorted off the property unless she wanted to register for an illness or injury.

"What is taking so long?" she shouted from the front.

Security walked down the hall and confronted the girl. I wish you could have been there to see her throw this gigantic temper tantrum. She threw herself on the floor and screamed, and once security tried to lift her, she tried to stab one of the guards with a nail file.

I called 911 and the girl was arrested.

Guess she got a room after all.

-K.W.-E.
Florida

Roaming

Many years ago, before tightened security procedures and such, our dementia wing was on the second floor and patients were simply monitored by head counts.

I'm still not sure how we accounted for all patients, but we didn't realize we were wrong until the next head count an hour later. We realized Mrs. Smith, a sweet old woman in her late 90s, was missing.

We searched the hospital high and low, but it wasn't until 45 minutes later that two officers arrived at the ER. Our floor supervisor was called downstairs to meet them, and she took me along because I had confirmed the head counts both times.

"Is she one of yours?" an officer asked.

Indeed, the frail old woman standing between the officers, wrapped in a blanket and shivering, was Mrs. Smith.

"Yeah," the officer said, "she caused quite an uproar. She wandered into the video store, got naked, and peed in their soda cooler."

The hospital escaped a lawsuit and had to buy the video rental store a new soda cooler. Additionally, the hospital implemented new security procedures for high-risk wings and developed a new system for head counts.

Thankfully, I didn't get in any major trouble. The hospital said they couldn't punish me for flaws in their procedures.

-J.T.

New York

"I could tell you were a medical family," the school nurse told me when I went to pick up my 5-year-old daughter.

When I asked why, the nurse said my daughter came to her office and announced, "I think I'm impacted because I can't have a bowel movement."

My daughter wasn't impacted. She was just constipated because my husband let the kids split a block of cheddar cheese the night before. Thanks, love.

-O.W.
Louisiana

Holy Moly

My position at the SNF was Director of Sales. It still sounds morbid to me to think of 'selling' slots in a nursing home, but it paid the bills and I did my best to highlight our facility's exceptional staff and facility amenities, such as our gaming room, television/sitting room, dining center, and our garden areas. As you can tell, we were not quite the SNF you'd imagine for bed-ridden, terminally ill elderly patients, but instead were more of a retirement facility that offered nursing care.

Anyway, I was guiding a tour that day. I had about 12 family members and potential residents in my group, which certainly made it one of my largest groups ever.

We toured the common areas of the facility and finally headed to see some of our rooms. Some residents could purchase what I called 'mini-apartments,' which were set up for solitary residency and were furnished with sofas, televisions, and full bedroom sets.

Small cats and dogs under 20 pounds were also accepted in these rooms. These rooms were considered 'luxury' rooms and cost a substantial amount more in enrollment fees and monthly rent.

We then moved to learn about our basic rooms, which would be what you would imagine when you consider SNFs. These rooms were set up with two specialty beds that could be adjusted via internal airflow. Under the top layer of fabric were tiny ceramic beads that aided in heat distribution and comfort levels. We were very happy to have these beds in our facility because they were high quality and offered our residents great comfort.

Well, I was demonstrating the beds and still have no idea what happened, but out of nowhere the bed practically exploded and sent ceramic beads flying all over. My potential residents and their families were trying to shield themselves from the beads, and most people were screaming. I managed to turn the bed off and tried to approach the group, but there were so many beads on the floor.

I'm not exaggerating: the scene looked like something straight out of a cartoon. We were all sliding all over the place, losing our footing and falling over.

Thankfully, the manufacturer compensated group members and our facility, and they offered a free replacement bed. I don't exactly know what caused this old bed to 'explode,' but we were assured that it was an isolated incident.

Understandably, some of our group members decided that our facility was not right for them or their family members, but we did enroll two residents from the group, and we made sure they were happy and comfortable during their time at our facility.

I don't think I'll ever be able to forget what happened that day.

-M.H.
California

Bite to Eat

Up on Med/Surg, we roomed two recovering patients because they were both quiet LOLs and we figured they'd both get more rest with a roommate their own age, as opposed to placing them with some of our other much younger patients.

Well, lunchtime rolled around and one of the women, Jane, could not find her teeth. She swore she placed them on the nightstand after breakfast, but then she started saying that her granddaughter had visited that morning and her great-granddaughter may have been playing with them and took them when the family left.

We searched the room and then went to call Jane's granddaughter. Jane's granddaughter couldn't find the teeth, so we really didn't know what to do. Jane was agitated that she couldn't have the chicken and dumplings that were being served for lunch, but she eventually settled on pudding after we swore that we'd save her some of the main course and she could have it after we found her teeth.

I just happened to look over and see that Joan, Jane's roommate, appeared to be having difficulties eating lunch.

"Joan," I asked, "is everything okay?"

She nodded, but I could tell something was up.

"Joan," I asked, "can you open your mouth for me, please?"

She opened as wide as she could, and I noticed that she'd shoved Jane's teeth in her mouth!

I tried to convince Joan to 'spit out' Jane's teeth, but she refused. When I gently tried to get the teeth out of her mouth, she repeatedly stabbed me with her spork.

It took three nurses to get Jane's teeth back from Joan, and I had to go to the ER for stitches.

Once we explained the incident to Jane's family, her granddaughter requested that we move Jane to another room. We complied.

We also spoke with Joan and her family, whom of which were extremely troubled by this behavior and stated that these types of violent outburst and out of character behaviors were becoming more common lately.

Somehow, everyone had missed that Joan had a severe UTI. Once treated for that and once her meds were recalibrated, she was the nicest, most polite LOL we could ask for.

-C.A.

Arkansas

Dance Crew

I was prepping a patient for emergency surgery and didn't have time to refill our prep room bottle with soap, so I was carrying a gallon jug of liquid anti-bacterial soap back to the shelf. I was nervous because I had never been involved with an emergency surgery like this, so I freaked out and dropped this huge jug of soap. The puddle started at the center of the room and kept expanding until it touched the wall.

Luckily, the patient was unconscious. I thought I could hurry and clean up the mess and nobody would ever know, so I pulled a bunch of towels from the prep cabinets and threw them over some of the soap. I realized I needed more towels, so I grabbed more.

I placed my feet on the towels and scooted myself around, just trying to clean up this mess.

Well, I heard voices from down the hall, so I tried to move a bit faster.

I am such an idiot.

One of the towels was completely saturated and became all slimy and slippery, so it moved right out from under my shoe. I started to slide and instinctively moved my second foot off another towel, and before I even knew it, I was slip-sliding all over the prep room. During that time, I could've made big bucks as a backup dancer... if the music was the Benny Hill theme song. Right as the door opened, an orderly and the patient's nurse saw my legs slide apart, and I did a painful version of the splits.

Holy hell, that hurt! I heard a pop before I felt the pain, but as soon as the pain kicked in, I couldn't help but to cry. The orderly and nurse tried to help me up, but it hurt to even stand. They had to get a wheelchair and wheel me to the ED.

I'll spare the intimate details, but I had to go to prolotherapy after it was determined that I suffered from a severe ligament injury.

I was not disciplined for anything, but I was lectured upon the importance of calling someone for help and working as a team. My story actually made it into our department's safety lecture a few months later. The slide said, 'Anonymous Employee,' but everyone knew it was me.

-M.N.

Kentucky

<u>Dire Emergency</u>

We were all relaxing at our station after a rough patch, when we heard a male shouting from the ES lobby. At the time, we did not have a security department, so as we suspected the male up front was unruly, I was chosen to go see what was the matter. (I'm 6'7" and nobody ever messes with me.)

When I got to the lobby, a woman was standing near the entrance, sobbing. Her male companion was at the receptionist's desk, screaming in intelligible panic.

"Sir," I said in a deep, loud voice, "what seems to be the problem?"

The man pointed to the receptionist and shouted, "She won't hurry up!"

"She has to sign you in first," I explained. "In order to do that, though, she needs to be able to understand you. Take a few deep breaths and try to tell me what's going on."

It took three times of him choking on air to take one smooth inhalation, and when he finally did, it was like he'd taken a two-second pause and went right back to flipping his lid. He was so hysterical that you'd think he just chopped his leg off or something.

"Ma'am," I asked his companion, "can you explain why he's so upset?"

She tried, but we had a more difficult time understanding her than her companion. I was close to giving up.

"The condom!" the male screeched.

"What about the condom?" asked the receptionist. "Is it stuck somewhere?"

"No!" shouted the male. "Are you stupid?"

"Sir," I warned, "please don't speak to our staff in that tone."

"Well," the male said defensively, "nobody in history has ever lost a condom. Don't ask stupid questions."

"Tell me about the condom," I said.

The man started to panic again, but finally blurted out, "It broke!"

"The condom broke? Is that all?" I asked.

"You need to clean her out," the male demanded. "You really need to do something."

"Sir," I said, before he interrupted me.

"We already have five kids!" he yelled. "I can't do it. I can't have another kid. You need to do something!"

The male began to hyperventilate, and he passed out on the lobby floor. All it took was popping a salt for him to come to, but he picked up his panicked state right where he left off. He had to register for a panic attack.

In my head, I already knew there weren't a lot of options for the couple as far as their initial complaint was concerned. I figured the doctor would write the female a prescription for the new Plan B pill and then discuss birth control options.

The doctor went in the room, was in there about five minutes, and came out shaking his head.

"What's the matter?" someone asked.

"It didn't break tonight."

"Huh?" I asked.

The doctor explained, "She's nine weeks already and he just found out about it."

Well, that brought a whole new meaning to the male's please to 'clean out' his companion.

Our doctor connected the couple with our resources team to assist them in exploring their options regarding the pregnancy.

I still don't know if it's a funny or sad story because I was laughing before I knew the female was pregnant, but after that I just kind of felt bad because the male was having a rough time with the news.

-B.D.

Kansas

You Can Bank on It

I work on our mental health floor, and on our floor, visitors must follow a strict list of rules to gain access to our unit's visiting areas. As expected, certain items must never be brought on our unit. Examples of these items may include weapons, unauthorized medications, drugs, and/or alcohol. You would be surprised, however, how often visitors will show up with these items, either hidden on their person or being carried in plain sight.

All visitors are required to pass through a metal detector arch prior to entering the visiting area, and we've found visitors to be carrying knives, knitting needles, bleach wipes, family-sized bottles of alcohol-based mouthwash, alcohol, sex toys, fast food…We've seen it all.

One day, Mr. Smith's wife dropped by for visiting hours. She was walking kind of funny, but I just thought she hurt herself or something like that.

Well, when she passed through the metal detector, the alarm sounded. Per protocol, we asked Mrs. Smith to empty the contents of her pockets into a small plastic bin and then step through the arch again.

On her second way through, the alarm sounded. We started thinking that maybe her new jacket was setting off the alarm, so we asked her to remove it. However, when she walked through a third time, the alarm still sounded.

She seemed nervous about something, so instead of beating around the bush, I just asked, "Jane, are you trying to conceal something?"

She broke down in tears and nodded.

"What is it?" I asked.

I never thought to ask, "Where is it?" That would have been more helpful.

After a few moments, we learned Mrs. Smith had wrapped a miniature metal piggy bank in saran wrap and shoved it up her hoo-hah.

"Why would you do that?" I asked.

She cried, "Because it means a lot to him and he asked if I could sneak it in."

"But that's not something that's on the contraband list," I explained. "You could have just carried it in."

"Really?" she sniffled.

"Yes," I said, trying not to laugh.

I think it was the first time anyone had ever tried to sneak in something that was never banned in the first place. Unfortunately, I had to consult security, the House Super, and our unit supervisor concerning this matter, and Mrs. Smith was temporarily refused visitation. We did, however, deliver the piggy bank to her husband.

Oddly enough, once Mr. Smith received the piggy bank, his violent outbursts stopped, and he was much more cooperative with staff. Never did learn why the bank was so significant to him, though.

-D.I.
North Carolina

Long Way from Home

At 03:30, an elderly man entered the ED lobby. He appeared to be having difficulty breathing, and he also appeared to be having difficulty standing on his own. He grabbed his chest for a brief moment and leaned against the wall before he almost collapsed. We rushed to get him seated in a wheelchair and then hurried him back to a room for treatment.

While we were getting the patient set up on oxygen and grabbing his vitals, we asked if he was having chest pains. He shook his head and stated he was not.

"How long have you been short of breath?" the doctor asked.

"About an hour," the patient replied.

"Did it come out of the blue, or did it work itself up gradually?"

"Gradually," the patient said.

"Did it wake you from your sleep?" asked the doctor.

The patient shook his head and stated, "I was already awake."

The doctor joked, "I'm a bit of a night owl myself. What were you doing up in the middle of the night?"

"Walking here," the patient answered. "That's why I can't breathe."

"How far of a walk is that?" a nurse questioned.

"About two miles," the patient replied.

Well no wonder the man was short of breath!

"So you didn't come here for trouble breathing?" the doctor asked.

The patient shook his head.

"So why did you decide to come in tonight?"

The patient shrugged and said, "I can't remember."

We called his wife, who confirmed her husband left the house about an hour earlier and told her he was walking to the hospital for a complaint of ear pain. The patient's wife said he was of sound mind, but he's always been forgetful, and she laughed it off when we told her he said he'd forgotten why he came to the hospital in the first place. She said he didn't take the couple's only vehicle because in 72 years of marriage he's never left her without a car and when she said she was too tired to accompany him to the hospital, he said leaving her without a vehicle "wasn't something [he] was going to start doing now."

"John," one of the nurses said to the patient, "your wife said you came here for ear pain."

The patient let out a guttural laugh and said, "Oh, that? No, it doesn't hurt anymore."

His wife picked him up from the hospital shortly after.

-P.N.

Iowa

People, come on. When they say you can buy sex toys at adult stores, they don't mean you run out to Lowe's when you're feeling frisky. I really want to know the thought process involved in finding the perfect screwdriver handle to meet your sexual needs. All I can imagine is a man with a beer belly standing in aisle five and thinking, "Man, that's the one I want to shove up my butt."

-D.K.
Georgia

Sealed the Deal

I bought my girlfriend two shirts for her birthday and was so proud of myself. I brought them to work to show off my proud moment to my coworkers, who were always dogging on their husbands and boyfriends about always buying the wrong gifts.

Everyone was beating around the bush and I could tell they didn't want to be insulting, but nobody would give me an honest opinion either way.

I was growing frustrated, so I decided to put the shirts back in the store bag, and I figured I'd go back to the store after work to return the shirts.

The Alzheimer's patient returning from restroom with an orderly on her arm stopped in her tracks and exclaimed, "Those are some of the ugliest damned clothes I've ever seen in my life. And believe me, honey, I lived through the eighties with hot pink wind suits."

"Thank you!" I said to the patient, overjoyed that someone was finally brave enough to tell me the truth.

"For what?" she asked, markedly confused.

"For telling me the shirts I bought are ugly."

It was in that moment that I realized the patient had entered an episode and had no idea who I was, where she was, or that we had interacted seconds prior.

She touched my scrub top and said, "Yeah. Honey, that blue doesn't look good on you. You have too big of a nose to wear that color, and you could probably stand to lose some weight if you ever wanna get a lady. Or are you gay?"

The orderly laughed and said, "Okay, Mrs. Smith. Let's get you back to bed."

I had some self esteem issues for the rest of the day, but I'm grateful that someone finally gave me an honest opinion about the shirts I bought. I returned the shirts for a gift card to the store, which actually backfired because my girlfriend accused me of 'having no real interest' in her and only buying a gift card to 'take the easy way out.' Just can't win sometimes.

    -J.Y.

    Oregon

I was doing my nursing homework at the counter, where I work retail, when this woman came up to pay.

"What are you reading?" she asked.

"Gray's Anatomy," I replied. "I'm in nursing school and have to write a paper."

She laughed and said, "I didn't even know they wrote a book. You should just watch the show. It's a lot faster."

Facepalm.

-K.B.
Rhode Island

The More I Learn About People, the More I Like My Dog

I am a nightshift nurse and single mother. I didn't live in a bad neighborhood, but I can't say was a great one, either.

I own a lab/pit mix. Personality-wise, he's more lab than pit 99% of the time, but he's territorial of our yard and he would run the fence line and bark when anyone passed by. My house was the only one on the street that hadn't been burglarized or vandalized that year, and I know it's because the only impression anyone had of my dog was when he was acting like a killer in the yard.

For about a week, I had been finding food in my yard in the mornings when I would come home from work. I would pick the food up and toss it in the road and that would be that. My dog isn't allowed to eat table food, and he can only have one type of dog treats because he suffers from allergies and a sensitive belly. In addition, my daughter played in the yard, and I didn't need all the extra bugs or wild animals climbing over the fence to get at bread or ham slices or anything else I was finding.

It was a weekend when I got off work. I found some candies in the yard and I pocketed them and told myself I would throw them in the trash when I went inside. Of course, I totally forgot about them, so I took off my scrub jacket and tossed it over the back of a chair like I normally do. My dog went to his bed, and my daughter was just getting out of hers for the morning.

She was two at the time and was really starting to learn about going outside to play. It'd been all she'd been talking about for weeks, and I felt guilty about not being able to spend much quality time with her due to overtime, so I decided I would stay up that day and let the sitter go home, rather than have the sitter stay so I could take my usual three-hour nap.

When we were in the yard, my daughter found a candy on the ground. It was underneath her plastic slide. I took the candy from her and threw it into the road. We stayed outside for about an hour, and then we went inside.

I went to the bathroom and left my daughter in front of the tv for a few minutes. When I came out, my scrub jacket was on the living room floor and my daughter had candy in her mouth. I made her spit it out, but I noticed wrappers surrounding her and realized she had eaten at least three pieces. My dog was acting really weird and kept walking in circles around my daughter and would stop and rest his chin on the top of her head. He cried a lot.

My gut told me to take my daughter to the ER, but another part of me said, "Just watch her. You're overreacting. You're going to take her to the ER and they're going to charge you $700 for you to hear she just ate some candy."

Within 20 minutes, she was crying, vomiting, and then she went into a seizure, all in a short span.

I am a registered nurse in the emergency room. I keep patients alive when they're inches away from death. I offer comfort to panicked families. I didn't know what to do with my own child. I was completely frozen for what felt like several minutes. I think it was only a matter of seconds, but I still can't be sure how long it took for me to run across the street with my daughter in my arms. I banged on his door until his wife answered. She was wearing her bathrobe and slippers and looked tired.

I immediately screamed, "I can't wait for 911!"

She called for her husband, who raced us to the ER, where I had gotten off shift only a few hours earlier. I knew these nurses. I knew these doctors. I trusted them, but at the same time, I didn't trust them. They all became incompetent in my eyes. They weren't holding my daughter's hand like they were supposed to when she was sick. They wouldn't let me near her. They poked and prodded and raced around the room, but they couldn't give me answers to whether she'd be okay. They didn't even know what was wrong.

I'd never been a patient in any ER before. I'd certainly never seen my daughter as a patient, and I never, ever imagined this would happen. Nobody prepares you for this. Even if they could prepare you, all that information goes out the window.

Registration came in and asked me for all kinds of information. I couldn't even remember my own social security number because I was so scared that my daughter was going to die.

My daughter was transferred to a pediatric hospital. She had tested positive for **meth**.

The police department came in and took a report after I explained to Child Protective Services that my daughter had eaten candy I had found in the yard. I couldn't believe I was being investigated for child abuse, but I knew it was routine for anything like this. I still took it personally. Then I started feeling like maybe someone *did* need to investigate me because what kind of mom would forget to throw that out? What kind of mom would leave her kid in another room to have a pee break? I started questioning myself for doing normal things that millions of parents do daily. I was really hard on myself and couldn't believe that I waited to bring her to the ER. I couldn't believe I had brought drugs into my house. I couldn't believe that I had let her consume drugs. I hated myself.

The police sent the leftover candies from my jacket to a lab. They were loaded with meth. The police asked if I had found any other food in the yard recently. I told them about the other scraps I had found. Then they told me that on the next block over, two of my 'neighbors' had reported that they also found food in their yards. One neighbor owned a pit bull, and another owned an American Bulldog. The American Bulldog died at home and the pit bull was euthanized due to the drugged or poisoned food destroying his organs. The cops thought that someone was specifically targeting pit bull dogs or dogs they believed were pit bulls, especially because they had talked to other dog owners on the block and only pit bull owners had complaints.

I didn't know what to do, so a week after my daughter was released from the hospital, I talked to my ex husband and he helped me finance another place to live while I put my house up for sale. I'm thankful to know that while our marriage didn't work out, we are able to agree that we want the best for our child and will do anything to help each other out, if it's in her best interest.

I don't know if the cops ever found out who tried to kill my dog and almost killed my daughter. All I know is I have been more cautious with who I let see my dog because I don't want this to ever happen again. My new home has a privacy fence, in hopes that if nobody sees my dog, nobody will want to hurt him. It's cut down on how often he barks, too.

Most importantly, my daughter won't be an indirect target of some crazy person's (people's) attempts at trying to kill family pets. I still shudder to think what my life would be like today if my daughter didn't make it. To be honest, I think I would have taken my own life.

This incident did help me step in the shoes of my patients and their families, but all I learned was to be more patient with these people and understand that when things are happening, they probably can't think, just like how I couldn't think at the time.

-Initials and location withheld at request

Pinky Promise

My partner and I were staging, and we were so bored. I went to the back and put tubing all over my fingers and climbed back in the cab so I could make weird dinosaur/cat noises and wave my tube fingers around.

I managed to get all the tubes off except for the one on my right pinky finger. We got called to a code just as I realized it was stuck, so my partner told me to just cut it off.

I don't know what I was thinking, but I just it horizontally over the top of my finger, so it was still stuck on there.

We got to the scene and the patient was responsive. It wasn't a code; the people who called it in are the same people who told 911 dispatch, "Officer down" when an officer slipped on icc, causing 12 more officers to arrive within minutes.

We got the patient to the ER. One of the receiving nurses looked down and said, "You should really get that off your finger. Like right now."

I looked down and realized my pinky was purple.

Nobody could get the tubing off, so we had to cheat a little bit and do it the redneck way. I went to the bay and kept heating up a paperclip with a lighter and slowly burned the tubing in a line until I could get my finger free.

I couldn't feel my finger for a few hours, but it was eventually fine again.

I'm not gonna lie…I put tubing on my fingers back at the station to show how I got the first tube stuck on my pinky.

My mom says I'm a 'slow learner.'

-W.H.
South Carolina

Pecking Order

Everyone in our department (and most of the facility) knew Mr. Smith and his wife, Jane. They were an older couple who visited the hospital frequently, as Jane had many ailments and usually presented in bad shape and would require week-long admissions at a time. The couple never caused us any problems, and we offered the best care possible, as usual.

I still don't exactly understand what happened, but I know one night a registration clerk came back to our station to speak to the Nursing Supervisor. She said that Mr. Smith was in the lobby and that he was angry. After a few minutes, the Supervisor returned and mentioned something about Mr. Smith had received a large bill in the mail and was upset about it. I didn't think too much of it at the time.

The next day, Mr. Smith returned. I was cleaning the triage area when he stormed inside, stood dead-center in the busy lobby, and started shouting about how our hospital treated his family unfairly and stuck him with a bill exceeding $10,000. Security took Mr. Smith aside and suggested he call our billing department and/or his insurance company.

If you thought that would solve the problem, you were wrong. Security had to forcefully remove this 80-year-old man from the lobby. I know they felt bad about it, but Mr. Smith was disrupting operations and was upsetting our patients and their families.

The next morning, we were all catching up on charting, when I just happened to glance up at the monitors for the lobby security footage. I saw a bunch of our clerks, security officers, and patients chasing something around the ED lobby. A co-worker saw me watching and asked, "What is that? Is that a dog?"

I shook my head. "I don't think it's a dog."

We went up front to find about 20 people chasing a chicken through the ED lobby. It was a losing game, too, because most people had the guts to chase the chicken, but they didn't have the guts to actually pick it up. The bird was scared and angry, too, so when anyone would get close, it would turn its head and peck.

I couldn't even laugh about the scene because I was so baffled. Nobody could quite figure out how a chicken made its way to the ED lobby. Hmm.

Someone finally caught the chicken and security called animal control. The ED registration clerks had to call housekeeping, and they had to come down and clean the bird droppings and loose feathers from the tile. The mess did not seem like a big deal to me, but the hospital made a big scene about it and 'quarantined' the area because they stated chickens carry diseases. They rerouted patients through another entrance for the remainder of the day.

The next day, reports started trickling in that a chicken had been found wandering Human Resources, and employees on that side of the hospital went through the same rodeo of trying to corral this chicken.

Okay, two chickens in two days. No way this could be a mistake. We lived within city limits and chickens weren't even allowed to be cooped in the city, so I know they didn't break free from someone's back yard and end up at the hospital for a turkey sandwich or a job interview.

For the next two days, once a day, a hospital department experienced a chicken invader. I think after Human Resources it was Oncology, and on the fourth day that this occurred I know it was by Lab because one of my patients had just returned from Lab and was laughing his butt off. We all wondered why management wouldn't ask security to review camera feeds to find out how the chickens had been gaining access to the hospital, but we figured that would be the smart and easy solution, and when did management ever use their brains to get something done effectively and efficiently?

The last straw was a big deal, and that's when we learned what was going on. Mr. Smith drove to our billing office, which is located across the street from our main campus. He carried two large cages into the lobby and opened the doors, allowing 23 chickens to escape into the office. An employee called the police, and Mr. Smith explained to the officers that he brought chickens to the hospital and its affiliated offices to protest his bill and our staff's lack of empathy regarding his bill.

The hospital wanted to press charges, so officers arrested Mr. Smith and the hospital made a big to-do about the chickens in the office. They made all their employees work out of the main campus chapel for a week, while management sent crews to the billing office to replace the carpet and lobby furniture. Talk about overkill. I remember that being a big deal because they took Mr. Smith to court for disrupting business transactions, as well as holding him responsible for the extra cleaning required for the areas 'contaminated by wild fowl.' I really felt like they wanted to remodel and used the chickens as an excuse to stick Mr. Smith with the bill.

Details regarding the case leaked and I don't know how true any of this is, but I heard the bill Mr. Smith had received was what he owed after his insurance paid for his wife's care. I also heard that the hospital eventually dropped its lawsuit against Mr. Smith and wrote off his remaining balance following community backlash.

Beyond that, I'm not quite sure what happened to Mr. and Mrs. Smith because (understandably) they were upset and switched providers.

It's been almost 20 years, but I still can't see a chicken without thinking about that wild week.

-J.S.

Tennessee

When I asked my GSW (gunshot) patient for his name at bedside registration he said something like, "Little Taco."

"Your name is Little Taco?" I asked.

"That's my street name."

"What's your real name?" I asked him.

He shook his head and said, "We don't use those. It complicates things."

I explained that *we* used them, and we needed to get him registered. He reluctantly told me his real name, and it was a name that definitely would not have sounded as cool as his street name.

-L.A.
California

Giving Back

I want to share the story of why I decided to become a nurse.

I was rowdy when I was a teenager. I respected my parents and everything, but I lied a lot, too. For example, I'd tell them I was staying the night at a buddy's house, but what my parents didn't know is that my friends told their parents they were staying at my house. With our parents thinking we were safe and sound, we'd sneak off to a party and end up passed out drunk on a stranger's front lawn or in a field or wherever the party was that night. I don't know how I didn't die during one of those nights because I know I did tons of stupid stuff when I was at those parties. My friends and I were still in high school, too, so that just makes the stories that much more cringeworthy.

One weekend, we all wanted to go to a party, but nothing was going on. Instead, we decided to pay this old guy $10 to buy us all the cheapest vodka in the liquor store, just because we knew it wouldn't take much to get us drunk. I think a liter of the stuff was only six bucks or something, so you know the rule: the cheaper the vodka, the more likely it is to mess you up. Also, the cheaper the vodka, the more likely it is to taste like rocket fuel.

My friends and I split this huge bottle four ways and were hammered. We got the bright idea to go play mailbox ball. I don't know what other people called it when they were growing up, but it's when you ride in the back of a pickup truck and take turns using a baseball bat to knock mailboxes off their bases. Don't worry, the person driving was completely sober.

Well, after about 30 minutes of watching my friends smash all these boxes, it was my turn. I was freezing because it was mid-October and we'd been speeding through the country in the middle of the night, exposed to bitter winds and rain. I remember not being able to feel my fingers when I took this metal bat from my friend. I also remember that because I was so intoxicated, it looked like I had about 15 fingers on each hand. I don't even know how I was still conscious at that time because I couldn't even stand up straight.

Because I couldn't stand up straight, I wobbled all over the bed of this pickup truck and banged my knees up from falling twice. On my third time down, I landed on my face and remember spitting out part of my chipped tooth.

Never one to give up, I stood again and prepared myself to swing at this mailbox up ahead. I drew the bat back and remember getting closer.

I took the swing, but I missed the box. Instead, the bat swung around and hit me in the back of the head. I vaguely remember going in and out of consciousness at that point, but I wasn't exactly sure what was happening. I don't remember feeling any pain. I do remember my friends laughing.

I also remember feeling a falling sensation, but since I had just taken a few tumbles I guess I thought I was just falling to the truck bed again. Wrong!

I fell over the side of the truck and smacked my head on the road. I wore JNCO jeans at the time, and if you don't remember these, just think of elephant bottom pants with huge, wide legs. Since my pants were all ripped at the bottoms from me walking all over them, my jeans got caught on this rail on the side of the truck bed.

So we were going probably around 45 MPH, at the very least, and I was hanging upside down from the bed of this truck, bleeding from taking a bat to the back of the head, bleeding from the top of my head bouncing off the road, and bleeding from falling moments earlier and chipping my tooth.

I remember hearing my friends yelling for the driver to stop, and two of the guys were trying to pull me up. I guess my dumb ass was resisting as they were trying to help me, so I pulled away from them, somehow got twisted around, and my face smacked against the rotating tire. I was so drunk that I didn't feel pain. I knew something had happened to my face, but at the time it didn't hurt.

When the driver finally stopped, my jeans finally tore, and I fell to the ground face first. The driver got out of the truck, ran around to me, and rolled me over. I remember that as he was screaming, I puked all over myself.

Cell phones did exist back in that day, but only one guy had a phone and that was yours truly. My first phone was a Nokia 6000-something, and I only got that because my dad got fed up and quit his job, so he let me have his cell.

Let me tell you about that phone. It wasn't fancy like all the cell phones today. It had two or three games on it, had a calculator, and I remember it had this app thing where you could calculate the conversion rate for different currencies. That was a feature that wasn't the least bit helpful to anyone I encountered in my hometown because we were all the way out in BFE and the most cultural sampling we'd ever had was dressing up in nice clothes to drive two hours away and eat at the new Fazoli's.

Anyway, I doubt the phone would have even worked because we were way out in the country. We didn't even have a chance to test it because we couldn't find it. I guess it had fallen out of my pocket while I was being dragged.

My sober friend was the voice of reason who wanted to simply go to one of the houses we'd passed, but we were all drunk and were more concerned with being caught for smashing all these mailboxes. Nobody wanted to move me, so one of my drunk friends stayed with me as I was practically dying on the edge of the road, while my sober friend and the rest of our drunk troupe headed back to town for help.

While I was lying there, in and out of it, I remember telling my friend I was cold. I then thought of being in a warm house, watching TV from the couch, and I guess either my body saw that as a trigger or I just lost all control because I pissed myself. My friend thought this was hilarious, and I remember him making fun of me.

By the time help arrived, I was exhibiting symptoms of frostbite and I had lost a significant amount of blood. I was also still puking all over myself, and I remember EMS talking about how I stunk of urine.

I was transported to our local ER, but they weren't equipped to handle a trauma case like mine, so I was transported to a hospital three-hours away via helicopter. My mom was freaking out so much that they told her she couldn't fly with me, and since she wasn't in the state to drive, my dad couldn't fly with me either because he had to drive my mom to meet us where we were landing.

The list of my injuries is far too long to send to you, and the list of all my surgeries, medications, and rehabilitative treatments is even longer. Long story short, I suffered traumatic brain injuries and underwent a craniectomy. I had to undergo reconstructive surgery because parts of my face had basically been grinded off when I smacked my face against the tire. Before I fell out of the truck and thought I had only chipped my tooth, I was wrong. I had knocked out one of my front teeth, and then I lost three more teeth when I finally fell from the truck. I suffered multiple fractures and internal injuries. They told my parents I had a better chance of dying than recovering and having a healthy, productive life.

My recovery was nothing short of a miracle. I spent nearly a year in the hospital and even after I was released, I returned for rehab. Most of what I know from the night of the accident came from hearing the story from my friends and randomly remembering tiny bits of details over the years. Sometimes when I'm zoning out, I'll remember a smell from that night or remember how my hand tingled or something, and I don't fully understand it because it's been decades since it happened.

While I was in the hospital, I became grateful for how the staff took care of me and seemed to care about me as if I were their own family member. I remember feeling scared and upset some nights when my parents couldn't be with me, and one particular nurse would always come in and read to me. I was too young and stupid to fully appreciate that gesture at the time. When I got a little better, we would watch TV together or play card games. I never had a chance to tell her, but she always seemed to come around when I would be lying there, hoping I *had* died. At the time, it felt like everything would had been better if I had died. I wouldn't be in pain, wouldn't be lonely, my parents wouldn't have gone bankrupt from medical bills and gotten divorced. That nurse really helped me appreciate life, as did other nursing staff throughout the ordeal.

I wanted to be that beacon of hope for others, so I studied hard and went to nursing school. My mom kept pushing me to further my career, but I didn't want to do anything else. For me, the caretaker-patient relationship means everything in the world. My coworkers are always amazed because it seems I can always turn the grouchiest patient into the nicest person in the world, and they always want to know what my secret is. It's really no secret. I just tell them my story and we bond through a shared experience.

-K.M.
Ohio

The strangest object I've ever seen used as a stabbing device has been a wapiti (elk) antler. No, the wapiti dd not impale a hunter. A woman and her husband were out at a tavern, when she caught him flirting with another woman. 30+ years later, I still have no idea how the antler entered the picture. All I know is that the husband came to us with an eight-inch antler protruding from his abdomen.

-E.L.

Northwest Territories, Canada

Untitled

I am one of many Britons currently living in South Africa. My team and I (comprised of fellow Britons, Aussies, and even a few Americans) traveled to this state as part of a program that aids rural medical facilities around the globe. I use this term lightly and will explain myself in a moment.

I must say, I have found your books to contain the most foul, horrific, and borderline offensive recollections that I have ever seen. However, I am hooked, and our team passes your books around after rough 18-hour days, just to find the slightest relief from the horrors we have witnessed. Quite frankly, when I began your series (I started with Full Moon Follies), I found some of the stories to seem outrageous. After speaking with an American trauma RN, he assured me that these events do occur. He also shared a few stories of his own. I did not know whether to laugh at the madness or cry from frustration. As a nurse across the sea, I can tell you most of what you recollect would never fly in my hospital. Do we tend to agitated patients or patients who dare cause a ruckus? Absolutely. However, I truthfully cannot say I have ever seen a patient go as far as to assault an ambulance or defecate on the lobby floor.

As I mentioned, our program offers assistance to rural medical facilities around the globe. I have traveled to nearly every continent and have bore witness to atrocities I have never spoken of with anyone except my team, our chaplain, and my therapist from home (when I am home, that is). These facilities are often found in isolated areas and their buildings are usually dilapidated, have no plumbing, are overrun with rats, cockroaches, fleas, and other pests that are vectors for disease. These facilities often cannot adequately offer care for their ill or injured, thus resulting in deaths more often than saving lives. I want to clarify that the countries we visit do have traditional hospitals that are clean and provide outstanding care to patients, but the facilities my team visit are often referred to as clinics or stations, and they are the only source of healthcare for many rural patients. In many areas I visit, common causes of death stem from dehydration caused by dysentery, lack of sanitation, and other illnesses such as TB. What happens is outbreaks occur and these facilities cannot provide adequate medical treatment because they do not have the resources. In just as many cases, the patients we meet cannot afford what medicines the facilities can provide, meaning they often return to their homes (which are often shanties in which they share close quarters with other family members), and they spread their airborne illnesses. It is a vicious cycle, and one that I am uncertain will ever break. More and more days as of late, I wonder if our contributions are making a difference. Then I have to take a pause and remind myself of all the lives our program has saved, all the medicines we have donated, all the vaccines we have provided, all the clean water we have distributed. To someone, I have made a difference. I can only hope that one or more of the young children I have encountered over the many decades I have been in this program do grow up to solve the similar crises that occur in the forgotten lands of our planet.

I briefly considered apologizing for my dreary 'rant' regarding the conditions I view daily, but I cannot apologize for shedding light on such a worldwide crisis. These countries are in desperate need of assistance. I have rocked a six-pound 12-year-old child in my arms as they have passed, and I have comforted the elderly who have no idea why they have lived while everyone has died and continues to die around them. I have remained in a room for the sole purpose of shooing flies from a barely-breathing patient, and with that I will assure you wildlife knows far sooner than humans do when someone is nearing death.

The story I want to share with you may seem just as dreadful as all the details of which I have just shared with you. Some may chastise me for finding this humorous, but to those people I shrug. I whole-heartedly agree with you that we in the healthcare industry must work with what we have and often find humor in the most morbid situations, or else we will be swallowcd by thc darkness we combat.

While we were staying at a (non- South African) facility, a young male patient walked five kilometers (roughly three miles) to reach our location. It was obvious that he suffered from mental illness in addition to his physical ailments. He complained of head pain, abdominal pain, and constipation x3-6 weeks. It was discovered that he was suffering from enteric fever (Typhoid fever). The patient stated that he was 'supposed to tell us' that he was the last of his bloodline. His siblings had died from various illnesses and injuries. His father still lived, but he could not complete the journey to our facility due to the strain the walk would have placed on his frail body.

However, as we questioned the child-like patient, he said that his sister walked him most of the way and then instructed him where to go from there. We didn't know what to believe.

We placed our patient in a bed in a room that contained five other patients. Though he was in a weakened state, he appeared to have a fascination with pranks. He would move our tools when we were not looking, would tell us we had a bug on our backs, and one week into his stay he played dead. We could not scold this patient because he wouldn't have understood, anyway. He seemed 'too far gone' mentally to have a firm grasp on the reality of consequences.

Unfortunately we lost a patient during the weekend. What is even more unfortunate is that the facility did not have a morgue. When we had deceased patients, we were instructed to phone a nearby ambulance service, who would then travel to our location and transport the bodies. However, ambulance services in the countries we assist are also encompassed in this crisis. There are often no employees (drivers, medics, anyone involved in the process), and if there are, it could be days before we see anyone. Because of this, we had (and in many facilities we visit have) no other option than to cover the body with a sheet until pickup. This meant our four other patients would share a room with a corpse for an undetermined amount of time.

One night, I was on nightshift duty. I had gotten only an hour of sleep and felt delirious as I emerged from my hut. I had discovered a snake in my hut earlier that day and found myself too afraid to sleep. My team members were all sound asleep in either our tents or the small huts constructed especially for traveling teams such as ours. A native physician and his nurse sat across from the latrine and played a game of cards. I cannot begin to adequately describe to you the pungent odor of death that lingered in the air.

I had entered the patient treatment area to do rounds. It was quite late, and the electricity had been coming and going, so I was using a battery-operated lantern as I moved through the room.

As I approached the back portion of the room, I noticed the patient in reference had turned on his side and had cocooned himself in his bedsheets. I found this particularly concerning and moved slightly quicker to check on him, as he had refused to cover himself throughout his stay. I wanted to make sure his condition had not worsened.

As I was making my way to his bed, I thought I saw the sheet that covered the corpse to my left move slightly. I quickly shoved the idea from my mind and assured myself that I was suffering from exhaustion.

Suddenly, the corpse sat up and moaned.

I knew I hadn't imagined *that,* and I was utterly consumed with panic. I screamed so loudly that I woke what patients were sleeping, and when I turned to run I ran my shin into a protruding piece of metal that was jutting out from one of the beds. I left a trail of blood from the treatment room, through the sanitation room (a room in which we kept buckets, hand sanitizer, and bottled water), and out the front door. The entire time, I was screaming, "Zombie! Zombie! Run!"

I ran *half a kilometer* away from the facility and woke most of my team members. They were most displeased.

Thankfully, the native physician entered the facility and discovered that the 'zombie' corpse was none other than my patient playing another prank on me. I had no idea that the deceased patient had been removed from our facility by locals, and my patient took the opportunity to scare the living daylights out of me.

I was sutured up and was teased throughout our stay at the facility due to the incident. Each time I think about this, I burst out laughing to the point that I am in tears. I simply cannot believe I was in such a panicked state or in such a state because I actually thought a corpse had come to life. Quite frankly, in that moment I believed we were entering the zombie apocalypse that we see in films.

Our patient stayed with us three more weeks, and then we noticed a young woman had been lurking around the facility for a few days. We came to learn that her husband was the provider for her, their two children, her brother (our patient), and the siblings' father. Unfortunately, her husband had fallen ill, and the family could not provide food for everyone. The young woman had tried to make money by prostituting herself. She stated she wanted us to 'get rid of' her brother by sending him to an asylum. She stated that she thought he would die of his illness while at the facility. That was a messy situation and one I do not wish to detail, if it pleases you.

Thank you for allowing me to share my story, and I would especially wish to thank other readers like me of whom have shared as well. I cannot reiterate enough just how near and dear to my heart these books are, and my team and I wish to thank you and all the other readers for giving us joy, even in times of despair. I will pray for your American healthcare system, as well as for all the staff members faced with the ridiculousness we read about.

-M.C.

I tried to free-jump out of the kiddie section at our community pool, hoping to leap out of the water and land on my feet at the edge of the pool.

That's the story of how I broke my nose, shattered my elbow, was banned from the city pool, and am making monthly installment payments to the hospital.

I was babysitting my nieces at the time, so my sister was not very happy that she had to leave work early to pick the girls up from the hospital.

-J.R.
Texas

Rest in Peace

Just wanted to let you know that my husband is stupid. I had just gotten our newborn down, and miraculously, our 18-month-old had crashed on the living room floor. It was the first time in four weeks that both kids had been asleep at the same time, day or night, and I was so relieved that I started crying.

My husband, the idiot, said, "Watch this," and tried to jump over the baby gate that was between our kitchen and living room. He cleared the gate, but he landed on one of our mastiff's hambone chews, fell forward, and cut his forehead open on the kitchen counter.

Both kids woke up and were screaming because my husband was screaming.

We had to take both kids out (in the rain!) so that my husband could have his forehead wound glued shut and get told that he broke his foot. Of course, I was the one juggling two fussy children while he was off relaxing in the X-ray room. All the coworkers I was happy to avoid while I was on maternity leave somehow figured out that we were in the hospital and bombarded me with questions about when I would be returning to work. I sat in our ER room and sobbed.

Get this: the doctor told my husband to 'get some rest and take it easy' for a 'few days,' so he tried to weasel his way out of diaper changes, feedings, and bath times for two days. He's currently buried in the back yard.

Just kidding! I told him if he didn't give me a break I was never going to be relaxed enough to have sex again. I'm messaging this to you from my phone as I wait for the pedicure appointment he made for me.

-L.E.

Nebraska

Our ER has a shadowing program where young high schoolers get credit for attending partial shifts at our hospital. After a hefty amount of drama between some of our patients, I was ribbing with one of the girls and said, "If you like soap operas, the ER is really the place to be."

The girl made a face and said, "Ugh. I hate musicals."

I don't know if *General Hospital* just isn't a thing anymore, or if I'm just too damn old.

-S.T.
Illinois

Such a Doll

In our ES, RNs take turns as registrars. They generally have one registrar at the desk per shift, except on weekday evenings, when they staff two. At the time, I had been an RN for eight years and was pursuing a master's degree to become a clinical psychologist (I was pressured into nursing and realized quickly that I didn't want to do it forever, but it took some time to go back to school), so this case was particularly interesting to me.

A patient in his late-20s to mid-30s sprinted into the building and pushed a patient away from the registration window. He was cradling a doll that had curly brunette hair and bright green eyes.

"Sir!" I exclaimed, as I tried to apologize to the patient he'd pushed.

"My wife needs help," the man screamed wildly. "I think she's having a heart attack, and she needs help!"

"We'll get a team to help you," I assured him.

I dialed to our station, but I was informed I needed to get a wheelchair from the lobby and help the man's wife into the building, as everyone in back was busy. Thankfully, the patient who'd been pushed out of the way had mostly finished registering and was easygoing.

"Let's go get your wife," I said to the man.

He tried to speak, but I inadvertently cut him off to ask where he was parked.

"Out front," he replied. "But that doesn't matter."

I didn't think anything of the statement. I just grabbed a wheelchair from the corner and opened it. As I turned it around to face the ES entrance/exit, the man shook his head and said, "It's okay, I'll carry her."

"Sir," I said, "I can't let you do that. It's standard procedure that we use a wheelchair."

"Okay, fine," he said. "Just hurry."

He then placed the doll he'd been carrying in the wheelchair and said, "It's okay, baby, they're gonna take good care of you."

I stopped in my tracks, looked the man straight in his eyes, and I asked, "Are you freaking kidding me?"

Not for one second did I stop to think before I asked the man that, that we were dealing with mental illness rather than just being 'trolled.'

"You have to help her," he pleaded tearfully. "I don't know how this can happen. She works out six days a week, and we do the paleo diet. She doesn't even smoke or drink."

He sobbed, "Please help her. I don't want her to die."

It was at that moment, seeing the expression of sheer panic on this man's face, that I realized he *was* serious. He honestly believed this 13-inch tall plastic doll was experiencing chest pains.

I did what I had to do, and I assured him he came to the right place and we would get his 'wife' treated ASAP. I took the man to a room and placed the doll on the bed. I told him I would be back with help.

Once I explained the situation to our Charge, he kind of laughed and thought I was playing a joke on him. He realized I was serious and said, "Well, we can't honestly be expected to treat a toy."

He wanted to call psych, but the doll's 'husband' kept coming to the station and demanding that we speed it up. To satisfy the man, Charge instructed me to enter the room with a tech and hook up leads to the doll. Charge wanted to speak to a counselor, but he wanted the man to remain calm until someone could come to ES. I was instructed to treat the doll as if she were any other patient in our ES.

In the room, the man insisted that he be the one to undress his wife. He stated that her clothes were expensive and that his wife purchased the clothes from a 'designer boutique.' He said the dress she was wearing at the time cost $225, and that she would never forgive him if he let hospital staff tear a hole in it or lose one of the pearl buttons. He tenderly undressed the doll and removed its shoes, which were a pair of flats made from some sort of jelly material. He carefully folded the dress and placed it on the counter, and then he placed the shoes adjacent. I was surprised to see that the doll was wearing lingerie: a plain, gray bralette and matching underpants.

"Does she need to be naked?" the man asked.

"What is going on?" the tech asked, bewildered.

I shot her a look and said to the man, "No, this should be okay. We'll work around her undergarments."

"Can she have a blanket?" he asked. "She says she's cold."

"She's speaking to you right now?" I asked.

He nodded hurriedly and said, "Sorry, she's always had such a quiet voice. She's kind of shy."

I paused but then said, "That's not a problem."

The tech had no clue what was going on, but she was sick of it and stormed out of the room. I heard Charge yelling, and then the tech came right back in and apologized. She told the man, "I'm sorry for how I treated your wife. It's just that…"

I could tell she didn't know what to say and felt awkward, so I helped her out and explained to the man, "Her sister and your wife bear a strong resemblance. I'm sure she was just flustered."

The tech hurriedly agreed.

We attached leads to the doll, but our machines obviously weren't detecting rhythms, so we had to turn the cart away from the man. He was breathing down are necks and demanded to know what the readout said. I told the man that the cart was not set up for printed readouts, and that the results would be electronically sent to our doctor's computer. I said it would take a few minutes for the doctor to read the results and decide a course of action.

The tech and I left the room. I was speechless. Even in mock sessions at the university, we never dreamed up this scenario. Nursing school sure as heck didn't prepare me for this. We all knew, however, how important it was to keep the doll's 'husband' calm. We didn't feel comfortable with him leaving, and we didn't know how he'd react if we didn't continue to go along with his belief that the doll was real.

In the meantime, we collected the 'patient's' name, age, and contact information. The man gave us his insurance information and said that it should cover the bill. We quickly determined he had a history of mental illness and had been a patient at some of our affiliated treatment facilities in the past. We relayed this information to the counselor upstairs, and she just said, "Oh dear. I'll call his mom."

In the end, the man's mother arrived at the hospital and she was able to work with our mental health counselor to convince him to sign in as a patient. He agreed to a 72-hour-hold, but only after we lied and said his 'wife' indeed suffered from a heart attack and would need to spend some time on ICU. I do know that the man was transferred to another facility shortly after, but I'm not sure how that came about.

Honestly, I don't think we'd ever seen a patient with that specific delusion before. We'd seen patients suffering from schizophrenia, who'd be hearing voices or seeing things that were not there, but never a case of a patient believing he was married to a doll. Or, I guess it'd be fitting to say a man who believed his doll was a living person.

-N.L., LCP

Location withheld at request

Had a guy come in once, and he said his tongue hurt. It was a tad bit swollen, but nothing to write home about.

I asked if he'd eaten anything new or had been using his tongue a lot that day.

He kinda just looked around. His girlfriend proudly announced that he'd performed an hour of oral sex on her earlier that day.

Ding, ding. We have a winner.

I told him to give his tongue a break.

-J.M., M.D.
Florida

The proudest moment of my career was calling social services in regard to my elderly patient's neglect by her caretakers. She told me her grandson was pocketing her meds, barely fed her, and that he refused to take her in to get new eyeglasses after he'd broken her old ones. I believed her, especially when she showed me how she'd taped two magnifying glasses together to be able to read the newspaper.

-T.S.
South Carolina

A Christmas Wish

I volunteered to play Santa at our hospital's annual Christmas party. Every department and our staffs' families are invited, so we always have at least 200 people at these parties over the course of a few hours. Santa's corner, of course, is a popular section of the room that is mostly reserved for Santa and his 'elves,' whom of which are also volunteers from various departments throughout the hospital. Kids can always take photographs with Santa for a $1 donation, and they're allowed to pluck a candy cane from the giant tree in the corner. It's fun for everyone, really. I particularly enjoy playing Santa because my only child passed away from cancer at an early age, so my wife and I don't have grandchildren. We made a pact to try to enrich the lives of children locally and globally, so we make several donations to charities and do everything we can to volunteer locally. I seem to be a perfect fit for the job and even have my own (real) beard!

I saw a young boy around the age of four or so throw a tantrum. I recognized his mother from our OB department. She was talking to a coworker's wife and in a moment of frustration, she gave in and allowed her son to run over to me.

This little bugger was so excited to see me. He practically leapt onto my lap and chatted excitedly about how he planned to leave out milk and cookies on Christmas Eve. He was no stranger to the happenings of the North Pole, and he was curious to know how the reindeer were doing and if they were getting plenty of rest in anticipation for the upcoming trip around the world. Chatty little guy.

When I saw his mom start in our direction, I thought I'd better hurry it along. She still looked frustrated. Overwhelmed, perhaps.

"Tell Santa what you want for Christmas," I said.

The grin dropped right off this boy's face and you would think that someone just told him he would never be able to have another dessert in his life.

"What's the matter?" I asked.

He was hesitant to respond, but he finally blurted out (and loudly), "My mommy yells at my daddy because his pee-pee doesn't work. And he says we don't have money for the pills. So mommy gets mad and goes to her bed for a long time and daddy watches football. So if you bring daddy the pills, my mommy won't yell all the time."

I didn't need a mirror to know that I had the most dumbfounded look on my face. Meanwhile, the elves were laughing their tails off, and the boy was just sitting on my lap, staring up at me as he awaited a reply.

The boy's mother walked up and handed on of my elves money for a photograph. She asked her son, "Did you tell Santa what you wanted for Christmas?"

"Uh-huh," he nodded.

"Did you ask for the fire truck?"

He shook his head.

"No?" his mom asked. "What did you ask for?"

"The pills to make daddy's pee-pee work!" he exclaimed.

"Oh my God," his mom said with a gasp. She looked away, clearly embarrassed. I was still so shocked by the incident that I couldn't react. My elves were trying not to laugh, but they weren't doing a very good job of stifling their giggles.

I tried to tell the boy's mother that it was okay and that it was nothing to be embarrassed about. It certainly was not the first time a child had spilled family secrets to Santa, and it surely would not be the last time. However, his mother was too mortified to remain at the party, so she scooped him up and carried him straight out the door.

I think it was about three months before the woman made eye contact with me again when we would see each other around the hospital.

-H.L.

Pennsylvania

Following a horrific accident that left my patient as an amputee of one arm and both legs, he joked, "I guess I won't be getting a bill, huh? I mean, I already gave you guys an arm and a leg. Consider the second leg your bonus."

-G.T.

Minnesota

Personal Problems

I've been surprised at the great number of submissions I have received regarding injuries to…sensitive areas, mainly the buttocks, groin, and breasts. Most have made me cringe. Oh boy!

• •

Dispatch notified me of a female locked out of her vehicle and added that EMS would meet me on scene. For whatever reason, she did not include more information, so I wasn't exactly sure what I would find once I arrived.

The parking lot was dark and empty, which was not surprising because it was 03:30 when I arrived.

I witnessed a woman standing near her driver's side door, sobbing and screaming. EMS tried to keep the woman calm, but that was not working. It soon became apparent that the woman had somehow managed to close part of her breast in her car door and her keys were now locked inside her minivan.

I moved to the passenger side of the vehicle and worked on unlocking it. The woman was in such a state of panic that EMS administered oxygen and practiced breathing techniques with the woman while I did my job.

A few minutes later, I was able to gain entry to the vehicle and EMS freed the woman. She was bleeding a bit and requested EMS transport.

-K.R.

Arkansas
■■

My patient came in with second and third degree burns to his abdomen, penis, and scrotum. He was crying as he told me he had gotten stoned and was cooking bacon in the nude. Grease began spitting out and he tried to move the pan from the burner, but he ended up spilling some of the grease on himself.

He was transferred out.

-L.G.

■■■■■■■■■■■■■■■■■■■■■■■■■■■■■■■■■■■■■■

Back in the 80s, we had to fly a guy out after he took a bunch of LSD, stripped down to his birthday suit, broke into a petting zoo, and got attacked by two donkeys. His injuries were gruesome. Aside from contusions, he experienced penile degloving. I don't know what ever happened to him, but I hope that incident taught him to lay off the drugs.

-E.C.

Location withheld at request
■■■■■■■■■■■■■■■■■■■■■■■■■■■■■■■■■■■■■■

The oddest injury I have ever witnessed was suffered by a middle-age man brought to our ED by his intoxicated friends. The three had been duck hunting, when my patient needed to relieve himself. He was also intoxicated. He placed his gun on the ground and stood to urinate. I guess his dog stepped on his gun or something. None of them were positive about what happened, exactly, but the gun went off and he was shot in the butt. It was a nasty-looking injury, but the man survived.

The most surprising part of this whole story was that none of the men seemed to be terribly upset regarding the injury. They were, however, upset because they hadn't bagged kills that day, and the patient's injury took him out of the hunting party for the rest of the season.

-J.S.

Nebraska
■■

My embarrassing story is that I had recently started dating a woman who'd been single for a long time, following an abusive relationship that had put her in the hospital for two weeks. She got a dog after that event, and she hadn't dated for three years, so her dog wasn't used to men coming into the house. I was okay with this and we worked on getting the dog used to male company.

Well, one night one thing led to another and she and I ended up in her bed. We'd stripped down, and I got on top of her. We started having sex and she was moaning a little bit, and I guess her dog freaked out and thought I was hurting her because he jumped up on the bed and bit me on the ass. I jumped up right away, of course, but he bit me again, this time on the inner thigh.

She had to drive me to the ER. I work in IT and know a lot of the people in that department, so it was pretty embarrassing. The ER said they had to report the bite, and the police asked us questions. The officer laughed and said they usually had to turn over reports of bites to the animal shelter for investigation, but he said he wouldn't because of the nature of the incident. The worst part wasn't even having to use a donut pillow for weeks; I had to explain to my boss why I was out of work for four days and then had to explain my injury until I healed.

I'm still dating that woman. We didn't punish the dog. Couldn't really, because he was just doing his job. As a precaution, we now crate him when we have sex.

-T.W.

ED RN here. It was my weekend off, so I had thrown myself a little party and had way too much to drink. I very clearly remember walking around my apartment in the nude, and pizza sounded like a great idea, so I threw one in the oven. Once it was done cooking, I cut it in half and took this gigantic slice of pizza to my bedroom, where I was watching old episodes of Grey's. I couldn't sit up straight because the room was spinning, so I tried to eat my pizza lying down.

Well, the cheese and toppings slid right off the 'slice,' and I was so drunk that I didn't feel the pain right away. It looked pretty bad and felt worse, but I was determined not to be a patient in my own ED on my night off, so I just had another glass of wine and went to bed.

When I woke up in the morning, I had blisters on both my breasts and the skin on one of my nipples had been burned off.

I was too embarrassed to ever tell anyone what happened. It took a few weeks to fully heal.

-O.H.
Florida
■ ■

I accidentally stabbed myself in the vagina by holding a knife the wrong way as I was trying to open a package while wearing nothing but my underwear. I had to get three stitches to my labia. Most embarrassing incident of my life.

-Initials and location withheld at request
■ ■

We received a pre-teen patient who was brought in by his mother. His penis, hands, and thighs were swollen. He experienced an allergic reaction while attempting to masturbate with a grapefruit. He said he saw something online that showed how to cut a hole in the fruit to make masturbation more pleasurable, but he didn't know he was allergic to his mother's breakfast food because in all the years he'd been alive, he'd never come in contact with it. His mom couldn't even remember if her son had ever had an orange or other citrusy fruit before.

Weird case, but the kid lived. I don't know how because if that would've happened to me at that age, I would have keeled over from embarrassment.

-A.Y.

Iowa
■■

<u>LOL @ LOL</u>

I am a receptionist at a very busy health clinic. Not only do we serve staff members within our employer's network, but we also serve the community. One would think we'd see more community patients on a day to day basis, but we actually see more staff members. I think a lot of that has to do with most of our clinical services are free to staff, so they don't hesitate to make appointments or utilize our walk-in hours.

During one of our walk-in sessions, a frail, white-haired elderly woman crossed the room at a pace I'd estimate to be a quarter of an inch per minute. She was barely able to lift her walker. Our waiting room was so full that we were out of chairs. People were standing along the walls and kids were running all over, but nobody thought to offer help to this woman. I kept trying to leave the office to assist her to my window, but my coworkers were busy, so I couldn't make it five centimeters from the desk without the phone ringing, other patients coming to the window, or the nurses needing something.

Finally, this woman made it to my window.

"Can I help you?" I asked.

"You're gonna have to speak up," she yelled. "Dropped my hearing aid in my tea this morning. Tried to put it back in, but the damn thing won't work."

I think I over-yelled, because half the waiting room stopped and looked at me like they were gonna catch some drama.

"How can I help you?"

"I need to see a doctor," she said. "It's a medical emergency."

"What kind of emergency?"

"I think I have a virus."

"Well," I commented innocently, "there are a lot of bugs going around."

"That's what my granddaughter said. I haven't been able to use my computer-box for a week."

I didn't think anything of her comment, so I worked to sign her in. She stated she could not fill out paperwork because her rheumatoid arthritis was acting up, so she asked if she could just tell me the information. I was able to get my coworker to cover my window so I could pull the patient to a private room, since we were practically yelling our conversation.

In the room, the patient sat on one side of the room, and I sat on a stool at the end of a counter, where there was a laptop for staff to use.

As I was entering my login information, the woman appeared concerned and worriedly asked, "Are you sure you should be doing that, honey?"

"Oh," I explained, "this is a computer for staff. We each have our own credentials, so we can access various information."

"Make sure to wash your hands," she said. "Are you taking vitamins? You should take vitamins. They really do help. Get you some Vitamin C. That does wonders."

I really don't know why I didn't catch on sooner. But when the patient said, "Maybe you could use gloves. I should've thought of that, but here I am," I just had to ask her what she meant.

"That's how I came down with this virus," she told me, as she pointed at the laptop. "My granddaughter said there's a virus going around on those dang computer-boxes. Wouldn't you know, day after she told me that I started feeling ill."

The woman went on to explain she tried to let her illness pass on its own, but she was feeling sicker by the day.

"I have friends on the computer-box," she said. "My granddaughter showed me how to play poker on there, and I talk to a woman in Sioux Falls. She probably thinks I'm dead because I haven't been able to talk to her in a week."

"Because you haven't felt well?" I asked.

She shook her head and said, "No, because if I get on there I could pass this crud to someone else."

She legitimately believed she contracted her illness via her 'computer-box,' and she believed she could pass it to her online friends.

I couldn't help but laugh.

Our NP verified this patient tested positive for Influenza and she was referred to the local ER for fluids and treatment, based on a number of factors and details of her condition that I cannot release.

Before the patient left, I explained to her that she did not and could not contract a virus from her computer, and that her granddaughter probably meant for the patient to be careful about clicking on emails from unknown persons or clicking on random links. Her expression was priceless.

-T.T.
New Jersey

In and Out

A first-time mother brought her newborn to our ESD at 04:00. She was panicking and crying as she explained that the baby's belly button 'just fell off' during a routine diaper change.

When I tried to explain to the mother that this happens in newborns, she became irate and screamed, "No, it does not!"

She demanded to see someone "who didn't graduate from a school that gives medical degrees to any idiot who drops money."

The mother lifted her shirt to show me her 'outie.' She pointed at her navel and shouted, "Mine didn't fall off! [His/her] dad's didn't fall off!"

She refused to settle down, and she just wouldn't listen to any logic or medical explanation of what had occurred.

We had to call security. Mom took the baby and stormed out of the ESD. She shouted that she was going to find someone who knew what they were doing.

Fine by me!

-O.S., M.D.
Maryland

The same doctor writes:

Once had a woman come to the ESD for white and red lines on her belly. She was seven months along with her second child. She stated she didn't experience this during or following her first pregnancy, so she was concerned something was wrong.

Yep, ESD bill to hear those were stretch marks.

I recall near the end of her visit she asked, "They'll go away, right?"

She was not happy to hear that my wife still showed faint signs 27 years after delivering our last child.

Bed and Breakfast

I was returning to triage after escorting my previous patient to a room. I passed our ER receptionist as she was running paperwork to the back.

"Have fun with this next one," she said with an irritated chuckle.

I thought to myself, 'Oh boy.'

When I arrived at the desk, I saw a mother with her teenage daughter. The daughter was standing next to two sets of wheeled luggage. These suitcases were almost as big as she was.

"Is someone going on a vacation?" I asked with a chuckle.

"I have no time for your jokes," the mother snapped at me. "I have a tanning appointment in an hour. Can't we hurry this along?"

"Let me just check my patient log and we'll call you back when it's your turn," I replied, trying not to let her bad attitude get to me.

"We're next. Don't you try to take someone before us. We're next."

"Ma'am," I said, "I'm going to check my patient log to be sure of that. Sometimes the receptionist's log does not sync with the nursing log, and—."

She cut me off by telling her daughter, "Get your stuff and get back there."

They stormed right by me and sat in the triage room.

I lost my cool as soon as I followed them.

"I don't know what type of service you're accustomed to," I told the mother, "but you don't make the rules here."

She told me to shut up and do my job. I've never wanted to slap someone more than I wanted to slap her in that moment, and that's saying a lot because I am not a violent person.

I took a deep breath and kept telling myself I would triage the patient and then move them to the back. I did not want to lose my cool again. I don't like feeling angry.

I couldn't even get to my work area because the teenager's luggage was in the way.

"I need you to please put your belongings outside the room," I said.

"I don't work here," the teen scoffed. "Don't you have someone to do that?"

"Well," I said, feeling irritated again, "patients typically don't bring a full set of luggage to the emergency room when they're here for…" I glanced down at my paper chart and then asked all confused, "cruise? What does that even mean?"

"It means she's staying here," the mother snapped. "And quite frankly, it's none of your business either way."

"Is that why you brought a suitcase?" I asked the mother. "Ma'am, do you understand that we don't admit patients unless they present with a true medical emergency?"

"This is an emergency," the mother said. "I can't find a nanny."

"We're not babysitters," I replied.

The mother rolled her eyes and said to her daughter, "This is why I keep telling you to marry for money. If you don't, you're going to end up working a mediocre job like this and think you can tell people like us what to do."

"Do you have a medical emergency?" I asked the patient.

She looked me up and down, made a face, and then said, "I don't have to talk to you. You're not a doctor."

I could have argued, but I walked to the patient to a room in back and informed Charge of the situation. Boy, I was heated. She knew I never get upset about anything, so she told me to sit next to her and take a breather. I have literally had patients throw bodily excrements on me. I've been hit by patients suffering from mental illness and overdoses. I've had drug seekers call me every name from here to Timbuktu because I wouldn't give them narcotics. I've never once had a patient or family member quite like this.

Charge sent one of my coworkers to the patient's room. Before I knew it, I heard the mother *and* daughter screaming as they berated my coworker and shouted about the service of the hospital. My coworker called security and Charge took over the patient as her own because she said she was done playing games and wasn't about to let anyone treat our staff that way.

I didn't have another patient, so I stayed in the back and ate my lunch. While I was sitting back there, security had to be paged to the patient's room twice, and then finally a guard remained just outside the door. The whole time, the girl's mother was screaming about everything under the sun.

Finally, about 25 minutes after they arrived, the mother and patient stomped out of the room.

"I hope you're happy!" the mother screamed. "You ruined my cruise!"

Charge shrugged and said, "Ma'am, the hospital is not a babysitter so you can go off and shirk your responsibilities as a parent."

The mother got in Charge's face and started screaming about how much money her family had and how the cruise she and her husband paid for cost more than Charge got paid in a month, so Charge just laughed and said, "Then you should have no trouble hiring a nanny, right?"

The mother replied, "I can't get a nanny because none of them will work for me anymore."

Charge shrugged again and said, "That's not our problem."

I learned that the patient's mother wanted to leave her teenager at the hospital for 60 days, just so the parents could go on an extravagant cruise. They managed to insult just about every staff member they encountered and behaved as if though we were all beneath them. They couldn't even come up with a lie that would warrant leaving the patient at the hospital. The mom basically said that nobody else wanted to watch her kid, so she was going to leave her with us. Based on how the mother and daughter duo were behaving, it wasn't the least bit surprising that they could no longer find a sitter. That poor child was only about 13 or 14 and had zero respect for anyone. I shudder to think of what type of adult she will become, and I can only pray that she grows to learn that type of behavior is despicable and won't get you far in life.

I have read all of these books and could tell you so many stories, but this one just takes the cake for me because I have never encountered anyone so uppity in my life, and

I've certainly never encountered this type of situation.

-T.W.
Maine

T.W. from Maine also writes:

I had this woman come in a few weeks before Halloween. She was dressed in a sexy lobster outfit.

I asked, "Attending an early costume party?"

She blushed, shook her head, and started to speak.

"Don't tell her. Don't tell her," said her boyfriend, clearly embarrassed.

She said to him, "She's a nurse. She's probably heard it before." She then said to me, "My boyfriend told me about a fantasy he had, so we were trying a new position and I fell off the bed."

"Coulda just told her you fell," the boyfriend said under his breath.

Poor thing broke her arm and the boyfriend went to the car because he was too embarrassed.

I still sometimes wonder what the fantasy was that involved her dressing like a lobster.

I work in L&D (labor and delivery), and we had a teenage couple welcoming their first child. They couldn't have been more than 15 or 16-years-old. As soon as mom delivered, the father freaked out and said, "I can't do this. Can't you just put it back in for a while?"

"Honey, the baby's out. There's no putting it back in anywhere," I said.

I thought the doctor was going to pass out because he was laughing so hard. The father *did* pass out when he got too close to the end of the delivery table and saw mom deliver the placenta.

That's probably the craziest story I have.

-L.Λ.-C.
Louisiana

That's Not the Right Word

My next patient was a male child accompanied by his mother. I called them to the triage area and glanced at the chief complaint, which was 'swollen testicles.'

We went through the child's medical history. I asked the boy's mother if he had recently been injured or anything of the sort. She said no. I asked the boy if he was in pain and he said yes. He pointed to our smiley chart and said that his pain corresponded with a five.

Then I said, "Okay, we're not going to have you take your pants off until we get in the room."

His mom flipped out and screamed at me, "Why would you need to take his pants off if his testicles are swelled up?"

I felt like this was a common-sense thing, so I just said, "So the doctor can see his testicles."

"But why would he need to take his pants off if they're in his mouth?" she demanded.

"Wait. What?" I asked.

It took a minute, but we finally figured out that his mother meant 'tonsils,' not 'testicles.'

She wasn't at all embarrassed. She just shrugged and said, "Whatever. I'm not the one who works at a hospital."

-K.G.
Ohio

That's Also Not the Right Word

I recently moved to Canada with my native husband, and though I have what I consider a strong handle on the French language, I sometimes become flustered and say the wrong words. Sometimes the words I say aren't even close to what I mean to say.

Luckily, most of my patients speak English, but some elderly patients find French easier because it's their native language and they tend to forget English during times of duress.

During an overnight shift, I was explaining to an elderly patient how I was going to administer a suppository.

I have no idea why my brain switched gears during this sentence, but I ended up telling my patient I was going to insert a goldfish into her rectum.

The patient laughed it off, once I explained myself. Her granddaughter, on the other hand, reported me.

-Initials withheld at request

A Scary Common Problem

I am late reading your books, but the story about the snake loose in the hospital really hit hard with me.

One afternoon, the registration clerk called me to her desk stat. Two heavily intoxicated men needed to be seen. They had each been bitten by a snake. The first man to be bitten was struck on his ankle. When the second man attempted to catch the snake, he was bitten on the hand. Both men showed me their wounds, which were bleeding, slightly swollen, and slightly bruised.

They brought the snake to the ER in a large tacklebox and said they thought it was a cottonmouth. Especially because of the type of snake they believed it was, we told the men to keep the tacklebox closed and that we would contact our local wildlife services.

"You don't wanna see it?" one of the men asked me.

"No. No, I do not," I replied.

"Ah," the other man chuckled, "you're one of *those* men, aren't you? You know, the funny kind?"

I knew what he meant, but I wasn't going to dignify his mocking with a reply other than, "I don't like snakes, sir."

Well, we were backed up, so we had to make the men wait in the waiting room until we could get beds cleaned. We knew cottonmouth bites could get real nasty really quick, so we rushed to get two rooms prepped. Not even five minutes later, I went to the waiting room and called them back.

Right there in the middle of the waiting room, at least four male patients and/or patient family members had gathered and were peeking in this tacklebox.

"You need to keep that closed, please," I said. "We can't have a snake wandering around the hospital."

The man apologized and closed the tacklebox. I took each of the men to their respective rooms and (once again) told the one man to keep the tacklebox closed. I informed him that someone from wildlife services had been notified, and that someone would be out shortly to identify the snake and then relocate it to a safe habitat.

Of course, when I came back two minutes later, the man had the tacklebox on his lap, and he was peeking inside.

"Sir!" I scolded, "If you can't keep that closed, I'm going to have to take it away from you."

He apologized and promised he wouldn't mess with it again. He closed the box and put it on the floor next to the bed.

The first snakebite victim began to vomit. This is common in snakebite victims. We worked to keep him comfortable, and we were on the phone every five seconds to find out what was taking so long with getting antivenin delivered.

I was sent to check on the tacklebox guy again, but when I went in the room I noticed the box was open.

"Sir," I said angrily, "I told you to keep the box closed."

He said, "I did close it."

"Well, it's open," I complained.

"It's open?" he asked.

I think it hit us both at the same time that we now had a potentially dangerous snake loose in the ER.

"Why'd you let it out?" I screamed in a panic.

"I thought I closed it all the way," he replied calmly.

I kept thinking, 'Of course this man would be calm about it. He's already been bitten, and he's so drunk that he probably doesn't even care that he's been bitten.'

I, on the other hand, am deathly afraid of snakes and I was stone-cold sober. I carefully inspected the room with my eyes as I made my way to the bed to give the patient a cold compress for his hand.

He made a comment about maybe if I played with snakes growing up, I wouldn't be a 'girlie boy' now. I politely informed him we were still awaiting antivenin and this 'girlie boy' would be monitoring him to make sure he didn't die.

I alerted my coworkers to the fact that a potentially venomous snake was loose in our department. As you can imagine, tensions were high and most of us were scared out of our wits. We couldn't accidentally rub up against the cord to our computer mouse or brush a phone cord without screaming half to death.

A man from a local wildlife services group came and when we told him the snake had gotten out of the tacklebox, he grimaced and said, "Oh boy."

Another 15 minutes had passed. My snake bite patients were doing well after we administered antivenin. They were both complaining of nausea, but it was better than them being codes. I'm sure some of it had to do with the fact that they were sobering up and the hangover was coming.

We were all still looking for the snake and our supervisor called in the janitorial department to help us look. It was a madhouse in the ER. We picked up everything off the floor—trashcans, footrests, computer towers—and put them on our work station counters. The wildlife services employee suggested doing this in case the snake tried to hide.

Room four's call light started going off repeatedly. Just ding, ding, ding, ding, ding.

"Will someone get that, please?" Charge called out.

I was nearest to the room, so I walked in the room to ask our 94-year-old patient what I could help her with. She didn't even have to speak because I saw it.

There was a snake, approximately three-feet long, slithering up the end of her cot. There was no way the patient could move; she had been paralyzed from the waist down for 20 years. I think she wanted to speak, but I don't think she could. I know she saw me because our eyes locked a few times, but she instinctively and repeatedly stabbed at her call button with her thumb.

I didn't realize someone had entered the room until I heard Charge huff and ask from directly behind me, "Mrs. Smith, do you need help?"

I don't know what got into me in that moment, but I hope it never happens again.

Without even thinking about it, I grabbed the snake by the head and its body was swirling around in huge circles until it realized it could coil around my arm. When I turned around with the snake in my hand, Charge screamed and tried to run, but she tripped over her own feet and fell.

I still had the snake in my hand when my brain realized this, so I started screaming, "Someone take this thing away from me!"

I am not a bit ashamed to tell you that I cried because I was overwhelmed with fear and the sudden de-escalation of adrenaline.

The wildlife services guy came over and started laughing. He said, "This is a harmless little water snake. This little guy can't hurt anyone."

I was still panicking, and I screamed, "I don't care what kind of snake it is, just take it away!"

As soon as the wildlife services guy took the snake, I had a full-blown panic attack. My coworkers signed me in and put me on a good ole' fashioned Ativan drip. That's the only thing in the world better than my Meemaw's pecan pie.

The entire incident was reported to management. I ended up receiving employee of the month. That honor came with a certificate, a few gift cards, and my picture in the monthly hospital-wide newsletter. In a way, I don't feel that I deserved that honor because I did not act out of bravery. On the other hand, I grabbed a freaking snake from a patient's bed, so yeah, I'm glad I got some kind of recognition for that.

-J.R.L.
Georgia

<u>Beary Scary</u>

In our ED, a RN will typically assist Lab
during a pediatric blood draw. We've found
the procedure to be much less stressful on the
patient, his/her family, and our staff if we can
distract the child.

When I assist with pediatric draws, I like
to grab a stuffed animal from our toy bin. I
usually hold the toy by the back of its neck,
which allows me to maneuver the toy's head
as if it is looking around the room or reacting
to the patient. I speak in silly voice and
pretend that I am the stuffed animal. I'd say
8/10 times, children are usually too focused
on the actual stuffed animal to know that I'm
the one running the show.

It was time to draw on a two-year-old
patient, so I grabbed a teddy bear from the toy
bin and followed Lab to the patient's room.
As usual, I spoke in a silly voice and asked the
child questions. I made silly sounds and told
elementary jokes. Before we knew it, Lab

was done. The child never cried or really even reacted to the needle.

I told the patient's mother I would be back in a few minutes to ask a few more questions. As I was leaving the room she stopped me, pointed to the teddy bear in my hand, and asked me, "How did you get it to talk?"

At first, I didn't realize she was serious. Then she asked, "How do you think it knew my son's name? Does it have speakers so it can hear who's talking to it?"

Once I realized the woman believed the teddy bear had carried on a conversation with her child, I excused myself from the room. I leaned against the hallway wall for a minute. I just needed to a moment to recover from that level of stupidity.

-K.R.
Indiana

<u>Old Enough to Know Better?</u>

I had recently emigrated and was quickly employed at a physician's clinic. I found it so terribly boring that I often find myself longing to return to the U.K., where I was employed at a busy A&E. Little did I know, the most peculiar patient I would ever encounter would come to this clinic.

Five minutes until closing, a female in her late-50s to early-60s entered the facility and loudly announced that she was experiencing a 'dire emergency.'

My first thought was to refer the patient to the local hospital, but I figured I should ask her complaint first.

She answered, "I have been unable to have a bowel movement for six days. I'm terribly constipated, and my best's advice did not work for me."

"And what advice was that?" I asked.

She explained that her best suggested trying canned pureed pumpkin as a remedy for her constipation.

Then she explained, "I'm dreadfully afraid it didn't offer a solution to my problem, and now I am stopped up and have glop oozing from my bum."

Rather than orally consume the pureed pumpkin, she inserted two tablespoons rectally.

We were able to supply the patient with a gentle laxative and suggested she bathe thoroughly to cleanse the pumpkin from her buttocks region.

This occurred some years ago, but I still find myself having a giggle at the patient's expense.

-S.A.

N.Z.

Point of View

Following a natural disaster such as a hurricane, it often seems one of the most common criticisms one will find is, "They knew it was coming. Why didn't they leave?" I wish to share my experience with you, and I hope it will offer insight so that others can practice a bit of compassion.

When I was growing up, it was never a secret that my mother was mentally ill. Everyone knew, and even if they didn't know my mother, all it would take was one interaction with her to know something was very wrong. Throughout my childhood, my mother was on and off medications. She hated taking pills. She said medication prevented her from 'free thinking,' which she has always (and still does) rant that the government does not want citizens to do.

Mom was involved in an altercation when I was about 12. She went to a mental health facility for about 90 days. She would not have gone if it had not been court ordered.

When her 90 days were up, there wasn't much anyone could do. My mom was never really much of a harm to herself or others, at least not in the sense that would lead to a mandatory mental health evaluation.

My sister and I were left to fend for ourselves. Unfortunately, my sister has a developmental handicap and has never been capable of making sound decisions. Even more unfortunate is that my mother basically let us do whatever we wanted. It sounds fun until you realize that I have been doing my own laundry since I was six, and that my sister, left without discipline or guidance, fell pregnant when she was 14.

Feel free to judge me because I constantly judge myself for this, but as soon as I was 17 I was gone. I received a full ride scholarship at a prestigious university and went on to study nursing. My mother was the sole reason I chose this profession. With me gone, my mother, sister, and new niece were left to fend for themselves, basically. My sister held a few odd jobs here and there; my mother qualified for disability.

After I left, my mother decided to move to Florida. She woke my sister in the middle of the night. They packed up the baby, filled the car with 'essentials,' wrote the landlord a 'see ya later' note, and drove down to Florida. My mom said to me, "It felt like it was going to snow, so I just wanted to be where the weather is warm." She moved in the middle of June.

My mother and sister purchased a home in Florida. I continued my studies, and my sister had two more children. My mom found a new friend in Facebook, which was like a playground for her mental illness. I had to block her for a while because she would send me 50 to 60 links per day, most of them crazy stories of how the government is corralling us for slaughter or petitions for anything and everything you can possibly imagine.

Fast forward a few years to a few weeks ago. Hurricane Michael was coming, and only a short time after the Carolinas were ravaged by another hurricane. My mother lived in Michael's path and was under mandatory evacuation. I remained in constant contact with her, so much so that I was written up for using my phone on the floor. Nobody seemed to understand what I was dealing with. They all said, "I'm sorry about your family, but they can leave."

Could they? Yes. Would they? That was too long and complicated a story to tell my coworkers.

I texted, called, and Facebook messaged my mother endlessly, urging her to evacuate. She refused. Luckily, I was able to convince my sister to leave with the kids, and she did. Sadly, this meant my mother was home alone.

My mother took to Facebook to post 16 back to back posts that were each several paragraphs long and largely consisted of incoherent ramblings about religion, the government, and how she 'trusted the universe' not to let anything bad happen to her. I worked tirelessly to reach authorities, but it was a sticky situation and there was not much that could be done. I do not blame authorities whatsoever. We all must abide by rules and regulations. By the time authorities *could* do anything, it was simply too late to act. They assured me they would check on my mother's residence as soon as the storms passed.

I cannot express how the guilt of leaving my family behind consumed me. Even though I had graduated from university, married, and had a child of my own, part of me felt guilty for living a good life and leaving my family behind to suffer from the unavoidable turmoil of mental illness and poverty.

My mother's Facebook posts gathered some attention from some of our extended family and from her 'friends.' Most of her 5,000+ friends don't know her in real life, and I suspect many of them suffer from delusions as well because they all share the same links about conspiracy theories and crazy rants. Some people were also urging my mother to evacuate, while others were assuring her that she was right in staying.

As Michael moved in, I lost contact with my mother. It was impossible to reach emergency services. I was transferred to several agencies around Florida and even somehow ended up on the line with someone in Georgia. I was basically told it was too dangerous out to check on my mom. Based on what I saw on news reports and webcams that were set up to face the beaches, it didn't look good.

The first day following the storm, I was able to reach someone from emergency services. However, they did not have the means to check on my mother. I learned from watching the news that much of my mother's area had been leveled. When I spoke to another emergency services worker, I was told that I should brace myself for the very real possibility that my mother's body could be found.

On day two, I was informed that emergency services had visited my mother's house. A tree had fallen on it and the second story of the home was a total loss. My mother's home was one of two left standing on her block. The team of volunteers found my mother's belongings, but they couldn't find her. They informed me that they could not check the rubble, and that it was possible that my mother's body was among the rubble. I cried and was under the impression that my mom had been killed. The emergency services team said they couldn't take anything from the house at the time. I thought to myself that there wasn't anything to take.

On day three, I picked up my phone and my gut told me to log on Facebook. I'm still not sure why, but I'm glad I did because my mother had gone back into her house for her phone and managed to post five long ramblings about how she was scared after the tree fell on her house, so she moved to her storage shed out in the back yard. Her storage shed is made of rickety wood and is in such poor condition that the city has threatened to fine her if she doesn't remove it from her property. Yes, my mother decided it was best to post on Facebook than to message me or reach out to me in any way to let me know she was alive.

I took PTO and sent my son to my in-laws' home. My husband drove from Oklahoma to Florida, where we picked up my sister and her children, and then drove as far as we could to pick up my mother, who was driven to our location by emergency services. It was a fight to convince my mother to come with us, and I was livid that she still did not want to leave.

She rambled on and on and on some more, and several times throughout the trip, I considered opening my door and throwing myself out of the car on the bustling interstate. I know it sounds bad, but I didn't want to give anyone the false impression that everything was suddenly sunshine and rainbows.

My mother, sister, nieces, and nephews are living with us for now. It's been a struggle, definitely, especially because mental illness doesn't go away just because times are tough. If anything, the stress has exacerbated my mother's mental illness, and it's difficult to sit back and not be able to do anything about it. Legally, I can't get her help. I can only suggest to her that she seek help, which is something she absolutely refuses to do and will always refuse to do.

I wanted to share this story with you because I think it's absolutely imperative that we show more compassion to others. It seems so easy to log on Facebook and comment a bunch of angry, rude opinions, but you don't always know the full story. Some of the victims of Hurricane Michael were like my mother. Some were living in poverty and had no means of transportation. Some had medical excuses as to why they couldn't leave. I know my sister only made it upstate because someone took pity on her. Had she been left to evacuate on her own, she couldn't have done it because she had three dollars left in her bank account until her next paycheck. I'm just saying that we don't always know why people choose to stay or if those people even make a choice to stay. They may desperately wish to leave but have reasons why they can't.

I also believe that our country needs to focus more on mental health care. Thanks to my mom's disability, she has been blessed to have resources available. Unfortunately, she chooses not to utilize these services. I think we need to educate ourselves more on learning the symptoms of mental illness and learning tips on how to handle our encounters with mentally ill sufferers.

So far, I have been able to convince my sister to stay in Oklahoma. We have been blessed with donations from my coworkers and from churches in the area. My sister has already applied for jobs through temp agencies, and they have worked with her handicap to find a job in which she can excel.

My mother, on the other hand, is hellbent on returning to Florida. I still don't know the details surrounding her plan, but I do know there's absolutely nothing I can say or do to convince her to stay.

-A.S.

Oklahoma

I clocked out from my 16-hour shift and went promptly to bed. I was phoned by our Nursing Manager two hours later, regarding a statement I had entered on a 93-years-old patient's chart. A coworker had reported my charting as a violation of conduct and violation of respect for patient dignity.

I *thought* I had typed: Patient rambling, often incoherently. Patient has obsession with clocks.

I guess the last 'l' I typed didn't register, so 'clocks' was in the patient's chart as a word that made her sound like a sexual deviant.

I explained my error, but I was given a written warning because I didn't proofread before saving my charting.

-M.G.
U.K.

<u>The 10 Reasons Why I Became a Nurse</u>

10.) I've never been fond of the gym, so I decided to go on the 'nursing diet.' I've already lost 11-pounds, mainly from never from having a minute to sit down, and never having time to eat.

9.) I've always wanted to try to beat the world record for being able to hold my bladder.

8.) I knew the only way I could prevent myself from blowing all my money on self-care was to find a job that banned me from wearing acrylic nails, nice jewelry, or needing a ninth pair of stiletto heels.

7.) I had too much of a personal life and a decent sleep schedule before. I need something that keeps me on my toes at least

70 hours a week, while getting a max of three hours of sleep per day.

6.) I was born to wipe butts, answer call lights, and bring patients extra pillows.

5.) I never did have any fashion sense. Wearing the same scrubs every day really takes the worry out of finding the perfect ensemble.

4.) I wanted to give up my social life, study until I couldn't see straight anymore, take a gazillion exams…just to be asked if I chose this profession because I couldn't hack it as a doctor.

3.) I never wanted to be able to socialize about jobs with people outside of the healthcare field, so I chose a profession that would have endless stories about puke, poop, and blood.

2.) I wanted front row seats to watching my tax dollars go to waste on a 32-year-old brought in via ambulance for a broken fingernail.

1.) I thought nursing would be a great way to meet people in my neighborhood. I was right. I see John 20 times a month, and I'm on a first-name-basis with Jane because she's here daily.

-H.L.
Indiana

A local retail store posted a still from their surveillance footage online, hoping the community could help find a pale-skinned woman who'd been caught shoplifting and later returned to rob the cashier at gunpoint.

We were contacted by a local tanning salon whose employees stated the subject had recently left their establishment.

When we located the subject, she was so brown that we could barely recognize her.

She told us that was the point, that a 'good spray tan can change your life.'

Not that much, I guess, because she still went to jail.

-C.M.
California

The Hunter Became the Hunted

I recently saw a news article regarding backlash a hunter faced for hunting. Something happened to me a few years ago. I've already shared my story with all my friends and family, so I figured I would tell you.

First and foremost, I believe hunting should be done legally, while treating the kill as humanely as possible. Many people these days do not understand that there is a difference in hunting humanely versus allowing your kill to suffer. I'm not getting into those moments when a wounded animal will run; these instances are often unavoidable and simply a part of life. I just wanted to make it clear that I consider myself an avid hunter, but I have morals and a strict guideline I follow. For the record, I do not believe in trophy hunting. I believe if you are going to take an animal's life, you'd better be using it for food and use as much of the animal as possible. Unfortunately, some people just don't agree with any part of that, and this story is about a few of those folks.

My 15-year-old daughter and I had just returned from legally hunting whitetail deer during shotgun season. It had been a great day, but a long one. Our area had been deemed a deer reduction zone, and as luck would have it, my daughter bagged a 9-point buck, while I ended up with a doe. We dressed the kills and loaded them into the back of my pickup truck before heading into town, where my buddy and I would finish the skinning process in his garage.

My daughter had been so excited about her kill that she talked nonstop for about 30 minutes straight and then the excitement got the best of her and she fell asleep in the passenger seat.

It was about 9 p.m. when I stopped for gas. I didn't think anything about leaving my daughter in the truck as I pumped gas and then went into the station for snacks and to pay the bill.

As I was walking down the chip and candy aisle, I happened to look out the window and see a man and woman grabbing my daughter's buck off the tarp. My daughter had apparently awoken to this, and she was standing between her open passenger door and the truck bed, hollering at the couple.

Without a lick of hesitation, I bolted out into the parking lot. The cashier called out to me, but I didn't realize I still had sodas in my hand until I was halfway to my truck.

My daughter was still screaming, and the man was shouting back at her.

I tried to approach the situation nicely, but I admit I was loud about it.

"Just what do you think you're doing?" I yelled at the couple.

They spouted off about how I was a disgusting person for killing defenseless creatures. I initially attempted to explain that whitetail deer were considered a pest problem to not only farmers, but drivers as well that year. It didn't take long to realize they didn't care.

My daughter begged, "Daddy, don't let them take my buck."

That innocent plea caused the couple to turn on my daughter. The woman involved ran over and got within centimeters of my daughter's face, and she was calling my daughter a 'psycho' and a 'murderer.' I don't believe in placing hands on the opposite gender, so I placed my arm between the two so that I could intercede. Nobody's going to get in my daughter's face like that.

At this point, the cashier was out in the parking lot, calling out to me to come in and pay. I wanted my daughter removed from the situation, so I handed her my bank card and told her to go pay for everything and grab herself something to snack on. She didn't want to go, but reluctantly agreed.

With my daughter out of the ruckus, I not-so-politely informed the couple to stop tugging on my daughter's buck. I knew I couldn't reason with them, but I tried to tell them we were free to disagree on the subject without resorting to illegal matters or causing a scene. I informed them that they were crossing a line by attempting to remove my property from my truck, and that I wasn't standing for it.

I thought the two were crazy before that, by all the uneducated nonsense they were spewing, but I didn't realize how crazy they were until the woman rubbed her hands over my doe's runout and proceeded to smear blood all over her face, clothes, and arms. While she was doing this, her partner or lover or whoever he was succeeded in dragging the buck from the truck bed, so now this buck that my daughter and I had guessed to be around 220-pounds was lying askew on the ground, while people were coming and going from the lot.

My daughter came out of the gas station and was in tears when she saw the buck on the ground. I told her to get in the truck and that I would handle the situation.

I stepped away from my truck for a moment and dialed 911 on my cell phone. I turned my back for half a second to respond to a passerby who asked if I needed help, and the next thing I knew, I heard my daughter let out a blood-curdling scream. When I turned around, the male was trying to drag my daughter out of the vehicle by her ponytail.

I laid into this guy like nobody's business. Lucky for him, some truckers witnessed me beating the daylight out of him and saw his partner jumping on my back. They rushed over and broke us up. We found out the gas station cashier had already called the cops, so we waited for the officers to arrive.

Well, the couple decided they didn't want to wait, and I was separated from the man after bloodying him up pretty badly. I was trying to calm my daughter down, when the couple got in their car and drove away.

They didn't get far because a few miles down the road they hit a deer. Their car was totaled, they had to be taken to the hospital, and the man was arrested for assaulting a minor. What really chaps my ass is that they tried to lie about what happened at the gas station. They even told officers that my daughter and I had pointed our weapons at them, which is something she nor I would ever even consider because we are and always will be responsible gun owners.

I'm not a nurse or anything. My wife works in a doctor's office and reads your books, so she told me I should sit down and tell you what happened. I can't imagine what the paramedics and cops must've thought when they pulled up and saw that woman covered in blood.

My daughter recently got married. She's still an avid hunter, but she's always been on edge since that incident, so I can't say it didn't have a long-lasting effect on her.

-K.D.
Indiana

One Tequila, Two Tequila, Three Tequila, Floor

I'll be the first to admit that there have been many times in my life that I have had a little too much to drink. Okay, *a lot* too much to drink. You just never know what you're gonna get when you imbibe too much. These healthcare professionals and LEOs share stories of 'Hold my beer' moments.

■■

My partner and I were staging at this 'Pioneer Days'-type event, where event participants dressed up in historical garb, bussed in blacksmiths and candlemakers, and cooked in huge cauldrons over open flames. There were a lot of horses there. Some were for people to ride on, and others were for show. One man was showing how horseshoes were made and how horses were fitted for the shoes.

The ale and wine vendor booths were packed. Most people weren't too terribly intoxicated from what we could tell. My partner and I noticed a group of rowdy college men, and it was clear they were heavily intoxicated. They were being loud and obnoxious, and I was just waiting for someone to ask them to leave.

Well, we saw the guys head over to a fenced area where someone was keeping two huge stallions. I'm not even sure I could have reached up and touched their heads because they were tall and muscular. They were just massive horses.

The guys entered the holding area, and just as the owner noticed and yelled at the guys, one of the guys ran from the fence and attempted to jump on one of the horses. He missed, and it was a terrible miss because he basically just ran face-first into the horse's side and bounced off. The horse didn't give a crap and just kind of looked around.

Well, a second guy from the group tried to do the same thing, but he came in at an angle. The horse wasn't having it, so it bucked, and the guy went flying at least three feet into the air. When he came down, the horse turned around and stepped on the guy's leg.

Our 'people observing' break was over, and we transported the idiot to the hospital for a fracture.

■■■■■■■■■■■■■■■■■■■■■■■■■■■■■■■■■■■■■

I read the story of the young nurse who was dragged to a party by her friend, and I have a similar experience to share.

My friend wanted to go to a frat party. I was almost out of nursing school and didn't enjoy being around wild people, so I protested. She guilt-tripped me into going.

While we were there, six frat guys brought out a kayak and placed it at the top of the stairs. They *set the kayak on fire*, got in, and launched themselves down the steps. About halfway down, the kayak flipped and some of the guys fell out and rolled down the stairs. Some were mowed down by the kayak as it continued flipping, and by the time it knocked down two end tables and busted a hole in the wall, only one guy was left in the kayak.

There were flames on the stairs, creeping up the walls, and the carpet caught fire pretty quickly. Some of the frat guys had pretty serious burns. Thankfully, a bunch of people put the flames out, but nobody wanted to call for help because they knew the university would get involved and nobody wanted to be expelled.

Once people realized that there were some serious injuries, my friend tried to volunteer me as a nurse. I didn't want to be involved, so I assessed the guys the best I could and told people not to move any of the injured guys and to call 911.

-H.L.

Location withheld at request

■■

We responded to a call regarding a burn victim. We arrived at the house party and were escorted to the back yard, where we saw a heavily intoxicated male lying next to a raging bonfire. There was a ramp on one side of the fire and a broken table on the other side.

I guess this genius did a bunch of shots and tried to ride a kid's bike over the fire, with hopes of clearing the table.

This guy flew up the ramp and through the fire, managed to catch his pants on fire, and smashed right through the table. He suffered from severe burns to his legs and broke his arm during the landing.

He puked in the ambulance at least six times and it stunk so bad that we had to go out of service to air out the back.

-L.D.

Ohio

▪▪

Dispatch sent us to a party out in the country, and it was madness. There was a three-wheeler crashed through the side of this garage, one guy was unconscious, and another guy had busted out at least four teeth and was leaning over, spitting out buckets of blood.

Someone showed us a video of what happened. The guy with his teeth missing laid on the ground, while the unconscious guy attempted to jump over him while riding the three-wheeler. It looked like the ATV was going to land right on the guy, but at the last minute it cleared him. But the driver fell off and landed on his friend. The three-wheeler flew into the side of the garage.

The toothless guy stood up and started spitting out chunks of his teeth and blood. Then he picked up a brick from the ground and hit the driver in the side of the head. The driver went down like a...pile of bricks. (Ba-dum-tiss).

Head injury, emergency dental surgery, and I'm sure someone got in loads of trouble for the garage being damaged.

-T.W.
West Virginia

■■

My patient suffered from a broken ankle, concussion, and a broken arm, which I thought was better than what he would have suffered from if his plan went off without a hitch.

Idiot tried to jump of a 10-foot ladder into a plastic kiddie pool. The ladder snapped shut and his ankle got caught. He landed on his arm, which was clearly broken because a bone was sticking out through his skin.

Wasn't even a party or anything, just a bunch of drunk people doing stupid stuff.

-C.O.

Florida
■■■■■■■■■■■■■■■■■■■■■■■■■■■■■■■■■■■■■

The plan? For my patient to stand on the swing of her daughter's playset and attempt to swing herself over the bars of said playset.

The reality? The chains broke from the playset and my patient launched herself into the wooden fence. She broke her nose.

02:30 911 call for that.

-K.M.

Colorado
■■■■■■■■■■■■■■■■■■■■■■■■■■■■■■■■■■■■■

Picture this: 04:00 on a holiday weekend. Said holiday has nothing to do with fireworks, and we are not sure why fireworks were involved, other than the parties involved were stupid and drunk.

Patient carried into ER by two friends. Patient had hole in his thigh and severe burns.

Friends told us that patient tied fireworks to aerosol bathroom cleaner and proceeded to light fireworks. Patient neglected to move out of the way, believing the fireworks would shoot into the sky and explode into a fireball.

Fireworks exploded on the ground. Aerosol can exploded, sent shrapnel flying at the patient, and set him on fire.

Patient was transferred out with a BAC .2+.

-T.K.
Virginia
■■■■■■■■■■■■■■■■■■■■■■■■■■■■■■■■■■■■■■■

EMS brought in a patient impaled through the neck by a 7-inch-long metal barbecue skewer, one that was on a long stick and is typically reserved for roasting hotdogs.

According to her friends, who showed up one by one as jail clearances for various injuries sustained by fleeing the scene, fighting with officers, and/or being tased, the patient was 'so drunk she could hardly stand,' was stumbling around the fire, and passed out, impaling herself.

The patient's wounds weren't as bad as they looked; the skewers went right through the fatty portion of her neck. She was, however, admitted to ICU for her alcohol levels, which were more than four times the legal amount...for someone who'd be legal to drink, that is.

-Z.E.

Ohio
■■■■■■■■■■■■■■■■■■■■■■■■■■■■■■■■■■■■■■

We responded to a frat party on the beach. Three rushes attempted to do flips from the third-story of the residence. Right before they were going to jump, the railing on which they were standing gave way.

One was brought to us with multiple fractures and critical head injury, one suffered from a collapsed lung, and the third one (the drunkest out of all three, of course) came out of it with just a few scratches.

-J.D.
Florida
■■■■■■■■■■■■■■■■■■■■■■■■■■■■■■■■■■■■■■■

My patient came to the ER with an entourage of friends. She was giggling as she told every staff member how she fell and 'shattered' her knee. She demanded x-rays, crutches, and narcotics. She and her friends had so much to drink that you could get drunk off their excretions if you were standing half a block away. She was showing zero signs of pain, laughed throughout the entire visit, and near the end of the visit she was having trouble remembering which knee she supposedly 'shattered.'

We got fed up and told her she needed to go. She had wasted all our time and resources on a weak attempt to get narcotics from us, and we weren't entertaining her or her friends anymore.

"So you're not giving me pills?" she asked.

"No," I replied. "But we will be sending a bill to your insurance policy's holder."

Once she realized her parents were going to get a hefty bill for her drunken drug seeking, she broke down in tears and then became belligerent. She had to be removed from the property by security, and then we had to call the cops because she came back and threw a rock through the ER foyer window.

-K.S.

New York

I could hardly feel my feet after attending my son's Homecoming football game, so as soon as I got home, I fired up the gas fireplace, laid on the brick hearth, and rested my eyes for a moment.

I didn't realize my feet were *that* close to the fire until I smelled something burning and looked down to see my fuzzy socks ablaze.

I stomped out the flames rather quickly, but I still had to go to the hospital.

I work on a burn unit.

-C.C.
Wyoming

Technologic Age

I work at a dermatology office as a receptionist and this is how my phone call went.

Me: Thank you for calling Dr. Smith's office. How can I help you today?

Caller, a female who identified herself to be a 20-years-old college student: Uh, I woke up and notice a mole or something on my hand. Is it cancer?

Me: We can certainly schedule an appointment for you.

Caller: No, I just need to know if it's cancer.

Me: Well, we'd have to have the doctor see it first.

Long pause

Me: Hello? Hello?

Caller: I just texted you a picture of it.

Me: Excuse me?

Caller: So you can show the doctor.

Me: Ma'am?

Caller: You said the doctor has to see it. So you can just show him the picture.

Me: Ma'am, the doctor would have to see you in person.

Caller: But why can't he just look at the picture?

Me: *Stays quiet*

Caller: Did you open it yet? Do you see how it's all brown and stuff?

Me: Ma'am, this is a landline.

Caller: Huh?

Me: This is an office landline. We can't receive text messages.

Caller: So you didn't get the picture? Hold on. I'll send it again.

Me: Ma'am—.

Long pause

Caller: Okay, did you get it that time?

Me: Ma'am, you'll have to make an appointment if you want the doctor to examine your blemish.

Caller: Does that cost money?

Me: We accept a wide range of insurance. Do you have insurance?

Caller: Insurance? Oh, yeah. Duh.

Me: Great. Who is your carrier? I can see if they're in our network.

Caller: Geico.

Me: Ma'am?

Caller: It's Geico.

Me: Ma'am, I meant health insurance.

Caller: Oh, I don't have that.

Me: If you don't have health insurance, we do require an office visit charge be paid upon arrival, but we can also set you up for a financial counseling appointment, which may qualify you for free or reduced office visit fees.

Caller: Uh, but can't he do it on Facetime for free? Then I wouldn't have to pay an office visit because I didn't come to the office.

Me: We don't do that, sorry.

Caller: Oh, okay. Do you know anyone who does?

Me: Nope.

Caller: Damn. Okay. Thanks. Bye.

-P.R.
Washington

Illegible

We had a patient come back after our incredibly busy shift had calmed down. He threw his script at me and growled, "They couldn't read that. They threatened to call the cops because they think I stole a prescription pad."

I recognized the patient as someone I had registered and discharged earlier, so I apologized to him and said I would go to the back and try to make it right.

I tracked down the doctor and explained the situation.

"Easy," he said. "Just give me the script, I'll take a look at it, and I'll call up the patient's pharmacy."

When I handed him the paper, he stared at it for about a minute and turned it every which way.

"What's wrong?" I asked.

He chuckled nervously and said, "I have no idea what I wrote on here."

The doctor personally apologized to the patient, wrote him a new prescription, and called the patient's pharmacy to clear up any suspicions the pharmacist may have had.

-B.B.
Ohio

I can't tell you how many patients we have come through our ER because they've been arrested and/or ticketed for possession of marijuana or possession of paraphernalia.

These patients come in and beg us to give them prescriptions for marijuana.

In most cases, even if we do write the prescriptions, we've heard it's not likely to help the patient because they didn't have the prescription while they were in possession.

-Initials and location withheld at request

<u>Mmm, You Said a Bad Word!</u>

We had this patient come through the ER one time, and thankfully it was only *one time*. She was probably in her mid-30s, decently-dressed…I mean, she wasn't slumming it, but she wasn't dressed in her Sunday's best, either. She had one tattoo that I could see, but she didn't have jewelry, except for her wedding ring. She was dressed somewhat modestly, but not covered from head to toe. All in all, she appeared 'normal.' When she talked, though…This woman drove us crazy!

When she registered at the desk, I guess it took over five minutes to get her signed in. Registration said the conversation went something like this:

Reg: How can I help you today?

Pt: I'm experiencing pain.

Reg: Okay, we can have a doctor see you. Where is your pain?

Pt: I'd rather not say.

Reg: Ma'am, this is strictly to decide which room to place you in. Are you experiencing vaginal pain?

Pt: (Gasps). Please don't use that type of language in front of me.

Reg: (Confused) Uh…Vaginal?

Pt: I asked you not to speak that way in front of me. No, I don't have that kind of pain.

Reg: Uh…

Pt: It's in my sitting area region.

Reg: Oh, like rectal pain?

Pt: I'd like to speak to someone else. I've asked you twice not to use that type of language in front of me, but you obviously have no respect.

Reg: Uh…

Registration handled the rest of the check in by apologizing to the patient, but the clerk told me she still wasn't sure what had irritated the patient so much.

Triage told me vitals went down like this:

Triage: Ms. Smith, it looks like you're here for buttocks pain today, is that right?

Pt: (Angry) I have already asked your staff not to use that language around me.

Triage: (Confused) What language?

Pt: You used an inappropriate word.

Triage: Ma'am, that's medical terminology. Does that make you uncomfortable?

Pt: I prefer to say, 'sitting region,' or my 'sitting area.'

Triage: Ooookay.

I thought everyone was joking when they told me about my patient. "She's just messing with you guys," I said. I thought, 'There's no way this is serious.'

Wrong, wrong, wrong.

"Ms. Smith," I said, "I'm your nurse today. I see you've come in for some pain on your buttocks, so I'm going to conduct an exam. We're going to have you lie on your stomach, and then I'm going to take a look and see what's going on down there."

I thought this woman was going to lose her mind and go on a full-blown rampage. She hopped up and started putting her clothes back on. She ripped her gown off like she was wearing a pair of Velcro pants over basketball shorts. There was a look in her eye that I couldn't quite explain, a fire, maybe.

"I have had it up to here," she shouted, raising her palm above her skull, "with this hospital's foul language. I came here to be treated, not verbally harassed. I'm going to file a formal complaint with the head of Human Resources!"

"Ma'am," I said, "what words do you find offensive in what I just said?"

"It's my SITTING AREA," she yelled. "I don't use any of those other words. They're filthy."

I calmed the patient down enough to conduct a quick (and I mean quick…I wanted her out of our ER) exam. The pain in her 'sitting area' was nothing more than a pimple. We took care of it, and then she made the comment that she didn't know she could get pimples there.

"Oh yes," I said. "It's actually more common than people realize. You can get blemishes on your back, face, legs, breasts, pelvic region…"

I was just babbling on and on, when the patient angrily screamed, "Ugh!" and hurriedly got dressed.

"I am done," she shrieked. "I am completely done with everyone being unprofessional."

I was so lost. "What was wrong about what I said?" I demanded.

She hovered her hands over her breasts and said, "They're called ta-tas. You have no right to harass me like this."

The patient left, and she did march her 'sitting area' right down to HR. She filed a formal complaint with management regarding harassment and unprofessionalism. When she told them what happened, and they double-checked with our staff, they basically laughed the whole thing off.

-W.J.W., M.D.

North Dakota

We Demand Whisky in the Break Room

My first phone call of the day went something like this:

Me: Dr. Smith's office. How can I help you?

Pt: Yes, someone told me if I cancel my appointment with you there's no fee, and it doesn't count against me. Is that right?

Me: Yes, ma'am. If you miss an appointment we do charge a $15 fee, and we add it to your record. If you miss two appointments in any 60-day frame, we will no longer accept you as a patient.

Pt: Oh, okay.   Well, I need to cancel my appointment.

Me: Okay, what day was your appointment for?

Pt: Thursday.

Me: All right. Let me just take a look here.   Hmm, we only have one appointment scheduled. Can you confirm your name for me?

Pt: Jane Smith.

Me: Hmm. Ms. Smith, I don't see that you had an appointment on Thursday. Is it possible you already canceled?

Pt: No.

Me: Okay, I'll take a look at next Thursday.

Pt: Okay.

Me: Well, I don't see you on there, either.

Pt: Well, I mean, the appointment was for the 19th.

Me: Of next month?

Pt: No.

Me: Of what month?

Pt: This month.

Me: You mean next month?

Pt: No. I mean this month. It was Thursday, the 19th.

Me: Ma'am, today is Tuesday the 24th.

Pt: I know.

Me: So you want to cancel an appointment you've already missed? Is that what you're trying to do?

Pt: Yes.

Me: Ma'am, I can't do that.

Pt: Why?

Me: Ma'am, you've already missed the appointment.

Pt: But I'm calling to cancel.

Me: Ma'am, you have to cancel beforehand.

Pt: But you didn't say that just a minute ago. You just said if I cancel it doesn't count against me.

Me: Ma'am, if you cancel beforehand, we can try to fill that slot with another patient. But since you missed your appointment, we couldn't fill that slot with another patient.

Pt: That's not my fault. You could've seen someone else.

Me: That's not how this works.

Pt: That sounds like poor planning on your end, not mine.

Me: *Sighs*

Pt: So I'm not getting a fee, right?

Me: Ma'am, if you missed an appointment the fee is already on your balance due by now.

Pt: But I just called to cancel.

Me: Let me look at your account.

Pt: Okay, but you need to hurry because someone's on the other line.

Me: This will only take a moment.

Pt: Okay. But hurry. I think Pizza Hut is calling me back.

Me: Ms. Smith? My records show you also missed an appointment last month.

Pt: Yeah. I didn't feel like leaving my house that day.

Me: Well, since you've missed two appointments, we're no longer able to schedule you. You will receive a formal letter in the ma—.

Pt: But I just canceled my appointment with you. You can't kick me out because I just canceled.

Me: Ma'am, would you like to take your other call and then call me back?

Pt: Yeah, I should do that.

When the patient called back, we played nice and allowed her to book another appointment. She missed that one, too.

-K.I.

California

You Always Find It
When You Stop Looking

When I'm not working as the ER unit clerk, I like to knit and crochet. On the last stretch of working overnights before my vacation, I went straight from work to Hobby Lobby to buy a new pair of scissors. I needed miniature scissors that fit with the rules and regulations of my flights.

At home, I took the scissors out of their packaging to test them out. I remember feeling lightheaded, so I thought I put the scissors on my coffee table before heading to bed.

I woke up much later than I expected, and I was trying to get my bags packed so I could leave the next morning. I couldn't find my scissors!

Boy was I furious! I searched the house high and low for three hours. I checked places you would never even think to find them, like inside the oven and refrigerator.

Sometimes, when I'm exhausted, I will do things that just don't make any sense.

Angry and out of patience, I decided to give up and watch TV. I figured I would swing by Wal Mart or something before going to the airport, and then I could just buy another pair to throw in my carry on.

When I sat on the couch, I felt a sharp pain on my butt cheek. Found my new scissors. Of course, my first reaction was to grab my butt, and I guess I hit the scissors the wrong way because they opened in the wound and sliced me open even more.

I put a towel down and drove myself to the ER. My coworker and friend had to give me six stitches to my rear end, and I had to use a donut on my overseas flight. Everyone looked at me like I was crazy. One guy was trying to talk to me because I was scared when we hit a bit of turbulence.

He jokingly asked, "Sitting on that thing so your butt doesn't go numb?"

I was stressed out and snapped, "I stabbed myself in the ass, okay?"

He didn't talk to me the rest of the flight.

My vacation wasn't as enjoyable as I had hoped because my doctor/friend specifically told me to stay out of the water for a few days, which totally killed my chances of swimming. I couldn't go horseback riding because I was afraid the movement would split my stiches. I mostly just sat outside and made a shawl for myself.

-J.R.

Connecticut

My wife asked me to disassemble our dog's crate and take it to the garage after he passed from cancer. I was carrying it downstairs and kept pinching my fingers between the foldable metal wires, so I shifted it around and immediately regretted the decision.

I accidentally unfolded it a little as I was shifting it around & tried to close it shut again, but I didn't realize I had caught my mesh shorts and penis between the two sections.

I fell down the stairs and knocked myself out.

My wife called 911 and they took me to my own ER for a concussion and a blood blister to the penis.

-C.G., M.D.

Location withheld at request

Nagging Wife

My wife said that I shouldn't get power tools because I 'didn't know what I was doing,' but I got them anyway. I cut the tip of my finger off. She said, "I told you so," and we sold the power tools.

My wife said I didn't need a go-kart because 'they're loud and they're expensive,' so I bought a go-kart. Flipped it two days later and broke my hand.

My wife said, "Just hire someone to clean the gutters, Mike. You're gonna fall off the roof." Well, I showed her…that I would most certainly fall off the roof. Only thing I suffered from that time was a bruised tailbone.

My wife said, "No, playing golf in the house is a stupid idea," to my friends and me, as we were doing shots of hard liquor at three in the morning. It didn't seem like a stupid idea to us, so my buddy teed off in the basement. The ball ricocheted off the brick wall and hit me in the face. Broke my nose and when I stumbled back, I fell into a glass coffee table and had to get 28 stitches to my arm/hand. Nicked an artery. Blood was on the basement ceiling, all over the floor, and all over the car. Wife's still pissed.

I swear, I'm gonna start listening to my wife more.

-M.Y.

Indiana

I tried to scare my five-year-old son by putting on a scary clown mask, hiding behind the kitchen door, and shouting as he came through.

I didn't realize my wife had come home, so I jumped out and scared her instead.

Out of instinct, she used a stun gun on me that she'd ordered off some website. I had been the one who insisted she carry something like that because I was afraid someone would try to hurt her when I wasn't around.

I had to go to the ER because my heart felt fluttery.

They kept me overnight for observation.

Won't be doing that again!

-G.S.

Utah

I forgot that my husband's SUV hatch door didn't stay open like mine did, so I flung it upward and tried to grab the 50-pound bag of dog food from the back. The door hit me in the head and knocked me forward. I hit my nose on the SUV interior and tried to stand up. I smacked my head on the door again.

My neighbor's teenager saw the whole thing and laughed his butt off. I thought for sure I'd broken my nose, but it stopped hurting after a few days. The back of my head hurt for about three weeks.

-S.M.

Montana

I Mustache You a Question

We had a guy run inside one day, just frantic. Half of his mustache was gone, and his upper lip was so red that it looked like he'd been burned.

He said he had a job interview coming up and needed to get rid of his mustache because he read online that he had a better chance of getting a job if he was freshly shaven. He said he didn't have a razor and he didn't have money to buy a razor, so he looked up on the internet how to make some kind of hair removal cream, and he let his roommate 'fake Nair' part of his mustache off.

He pleaded and begged as he explained that he couldn't go through that pain again, and nobody would respond to his texts to let him borrow a razor.

We gave the guy a razor from a supply closet we keep stocked for patients in need. I figured if anyone needed a razor, it was that guy.

He ended up coming back that night to be treated for chemical burns to part of his upper lip.

The guy was so mad, too, because he said the guy who interviewed him had a mustache.

-K.D.

Oregon

04:00 on a quiet, uneventful nightshift.

EMS called in report of incoming patient: burns to genitalia.

College kid said he wanted to see what his pubes looked like straightened, so he used his girlfriend's straightener.

He wasn't drunk, but he did say he used illegal drugs that night, and the kid was doped up out of his mind.

-Initials and location withheld at request

I Work Out

One night, we had a woman come in for pain in her buttocks and tailbone region. She was a larger, older woman, who was clearly embarrassed to be in the emergency room. She asked how long it would take to be seen. She looked scared when I told her it would be at least a 10-minute wait before we could call her back.

When she went to the waiting room, she kept her head down and would turn away when she saw other hospital employees. I thought it was weird, but whatever.

Finally, she was called back. I waited a bit, and then her nurse called to tell me she was going to be discharged. She said the patient wanted to give her information bedside, instead of coming to the front desk again for the discharge procedure.

No big deal.

I went to the room and asked for all her information. I had to ask for her employer and insurance, and that's when she started crying. I never even realized she worked at the hospital as a janitor. I guess I just never saw her because she worked days. She said she was crying because her coworker had walked by a few minutes earlier and had seen her in the ER. She was afraid everyone would know why she was in there.

I reminded the patient that we are all bound by HIPAA, and even if any of the nurses wanted to gossip, they could be fired and face fines/prison time for blabbing.

This seemed to calm the patient down.

She stopped crying and started laughing instead and said, "It was my own fault, really."

She went on to tell me that she had developed a crush on a man she noticed came to the gym when she went, so she was trying to show off. She said she wanted to show him that she really was trying to lose weight, so she'd really pushed herself on the treadmill.

She said she'd never done a workout like that before, so she didn't consider that her thong would rub against her skin. She was in the ER for chaffing.

We both laughed about it for a few minutes. I think it helped her feel better when I told her that one time I had been brave enough to wear a sports bra and a pair of spandex shorts when I went out to run around my neighborhood. My neighbor was walking his dog in my direction when my left boob decided to fall out of my bra.

We all have our embarrassing stories!

-A.Y.

New Jersey

We had a patient earlier who'd been tweaking hardcore, so I was trying to show my relief how the patient had been doing karate moves to the air.

I went to kick the air, when my resting foot slipped out of my clog. I busted my head on the counter and then accidentally knocked a computer monitor to the floor.

They made me pay for the monitor and wrote me up for mocking a patient.

-Initials and location withheld at request

<u>Showing Off</u>

We were having a department party at a local lake. It wasn't sponsored by the hospital and was considered more of a 'private' gathering that we'd invited everyone from work to attend. Of course, we had alcohol there, and most of us were fairly intoxicated.

Some of my coworkers created this sort of obstacle course. They started by shot gunning a beer, running through a zig-zag of innertubes placed on the ground, stopping at another 'station' and shot gunning a second beer, jumping hurdles made of beach towels and flex tape tied to sticks that were jammed in the ground, shot gunning a third beer, and then swinging from a rope and jumping into the water.

Most of us were involved, and most of us were shot gunning the beer by jamming a knife into the side of the can and gulping it down after that.

Someone was bragging about how they used to crack the cans open on their heads, and I, fairly confident that I could do that and make department history, tried it.

Of course, I hit myself in the head with a beer and almost knocked myself out. To make matters worse, I tried to walk off the dizziness I was feeling, but I stepped in a gopher hole and sprained my ankle.

I was a tough guy about it and just drank a bunch of beer from the sidelines. I was hungover the next day, which really sucked because I had to work a 12-hour shift. But, the party was fun, and we already have next year's planned.

-J.R.H.

Virginia

My Best Friend is Ativan

Trying to do a coworker a favor, I picked up half of her dayshift that ran consecutively following my nightshift. It worked out perfectly with my schedule, other than being exhausted.

It was the longest shift of my life, I'll tell you what. I should've known not to do it, especially because my nightshift was a full moon. Holy hell. We had mental patients out the wazoo. Even as the sun began to rise and new patients came in for the dayshift, they were just as combative and nasty to staff and each other. The extra security guards we had to call in for nightshift were bitter towards us because they couldn't go home when dayshift hit, as if we had something to do with all these patients coming in.

Fight after fight after fight. Overdose after overdose. Our mental health counselors were running themselves ragged. They even had to call in all available counselors in the area. I had to change my scrubs eight times during my 18-hour shift because I had been bled, vomited, pooped, and peed on. I even had a patient throw a cup of milk on me. Long, long night/day.

My four-year-old had an early release day, so I was parked in the pick-up line at her school. Just as she got in the car and buckled herself in her booster, my coworker called to see how the shift had gone.

"Let's just say my best friend is Ativan," I laughed to her.

I drove my daughter home, made dinner, and when my husband came home, I took a long, deep, five-hour nap. (Anything under eight-hours is a nap for me and always will be.)

My daughter went to school the next day, and that evening we had a parent-teacher conference/open house. We went to her classroom, which was decorated especially for this occasion. All the kids had drawn pictures of their families and filled out things about their families, like pet names and what their siblings like to do. One kid's answer to 'My dad's favorite thing to do is—' was 'fart.' That made me chuckle.

I was curious to see what my daughter had drawn for her family portrait. She excitedly guided me across the room and pointed to her sketch.

There was my daughter's stick figure, holding hands with my husband. My husband's stick figure was holding a book (he's a high school teacher). Our stick figure dog was off in the corner, peeing on what looked to be our new kitchen trash can (I don't know why he does it, because he never peed on the old trash can). I was off in the corner, talking to another stick figure I couldn't identify. I couldn't place anyone with bright red hair.

"Who is standing next to mommy in your picture?" I asked.

My daughter looked up to me and said, "That's Ativan, your best friend!"

I didn't know whether to laugh or be embarrassed or cry. I walked around the room and looked at all the other drawings and decorations, but I kept an eye on other parents who'd stop and look at the sketches. To everyone else, it just looked like my kid drew in an aunt or teenage sibling or something. Most of them commented about the dog peeing on the trash can.

Luckily, my daughter's teacher had great things to say about my daughter. She did suggest, however, that I be more cautious about what I say in front of my daughter, because apparently, she'd come to school that morning and told the story I'd told my husband the night before, about how a patient came in and masturbated (retold by my daughter as 'mashed potatoes') in the lobby and had to be restrained by security. (That was one of the calmer parts of my shift, by the way. We got that guy up to mental health in no time flat, and they told me the next morning that all he'd done for six hours was touch himself.)

The teacher didn't judge me or anything, and she said it was easy to redirect the conversation, but she just wanted to warn me that my daughter was repeating things like that.

-J.M.

New York

<u>A Message to Readers</u>

I'm not going to bore anyone this time around. Let's keep it short and sweet.

As usual, I wanted to thank you all for your continued support and comments/messages on social media. I enjoy interacting with you all, and I am grateful to have you all as readers.

Have a wonderful day, guys!

Check me out on Twitter!

https://twitter.com/AuthorKerryHamm

You can also find me on Facebook, by searching for 'Author Kerry Hamm.'

33757554R00182

Made in the USA
Middletown, DE
17 January 2019